REVENGE IS FOR GOD

Les Ray

Contents

1

My Inception

They say that if you don't see the book you want on the shelf, write it. We all possess a unique sense of originality and individuality. The story we know all too well, the story of ourselves. We all hold different stories, yet only some have more to offer to the world than others. He who has been at the brink of the abyss holds the power, the ability, or just the sheer perspective to explain life in a matter of mere words. Words of power, words that behold the truth. He, who is foreign to the darkness that exists in the world we know of, has not truly experienced life as it is. The reason I wrote this book? Simple. I have lived a life of wisdom and want to establish it as a part of history. I believe my story has the sheer power to open the eyes of the fortunate and to empathize with the unfortunate. Bad times are not a destination; they are just a part of this long yet not-so-long journey we call life. I want to show my readers that no matter how weighted their pain may seem, it's how we deal with it that defines our character. It is only when we begin to comprehend the tales of others that we are able to assess our own web of despair. My name is Leslie Ray, commonly known as Les Ray, though some of you would know me as Raz Ray, Raz-Coco, or Raz Raymond, and this is my story.

Born and raised in Edmonton City in Alberta, Canada, my father, *Cletus,* came from a small island in St Lucia, in the Caribbean. A small, beautiful island where my father worked as a waiter back in the '70s, just before the nation's independence in 79'. My father was a hard worker and strived to make a living, so an opportunity soon presented itself when my father's work ethic was noticed, and he was sponsored to work in a restaurant here in Alberta. All the while, my mom used to work as a babysitter in the city, helping to take care of her family. It was easier to immigrate back in the day, but it is nothing like how it is now. My father told my mom that he wanted to marry her and bring her to

Alberta. She was initially skeptical, yet agreed and was happily married to my father after her immigration here. Soon, I came along in the late seventies.

It wasn't long before the restaurant my father worked for went down under. Soon, he found employment as a carrier for an oil company, driving trucks for a living. He worked hard and was consistent but also had a sound mind for business, especially considering he didn't have any significant education. As we all know by now, you can have a college degree and still be an idiot. Anywho, he saved up from his job, bought a new truck, and started his own little business. Soon, he opened another little company and kept on going.

People love my father, without a doubt. Other than his commendable determination and mentality, he was just a different man. He was short, black, and absolutely loved old-school country music. He was a friendly man who got along with everyone I knew and had a versatile personality. His occupation required him to drive quite a lot, so he knew his way in the city. He had adjusted to the new culture quite well, considering a black man was a rarity at the time.

So, he was doing well with his business and was able to sponsor my mother's siblings when her parents passed away. They weren't the only people he sponsored; immigration was simpler, and perhaps as many people were not competing to get into Canada at the time, he could do so quickly. He was the first of his family to immigrate and gradually helped a big portion of our relatives, almost all of whom have families here in Alberta or started here in Alberta. He built everything out of nothing and deserves all the respect he deserves if not more. He worked hard for the people he loved and could manifest his desires by capitalizing on the opportunity of immigrating to a new city.

Elementary school was uniquely interesting because my sister and I were the only black kids in elementary school. However, this color difference did not quite affect us as children. As we all know, kids can be curious little devils because of their lack of general life experience, and so they are rather direct at pinpointing any *differences*. However, as children, we had a pretty peaceful time overall, a by-product of my father's efforts that gave us the platform to study and compete with the other kids. My mother, *Sheila,* supported him throughout the way and did everything from cooking to cleaning to mowing the lawn, you name it. She learned how to drive and got her license here in Canada after her immigration. She would pick us up, drop us off at school, and take us to soccer practice, and she was a fantastic cook and a beautiful woman overall. It's rare for two people who deserve each other to end up with one another, a rarity I witnessed growing up with my parents. Two different worlds collided;

my father's background was all a hard work ethic and responsibility, and my mother's side was merely giant male Oxes and strong, beautiful women.

My parents are lovely people who were accepted by helping the struggling people in the neighbourhood. Our families would often be a part of all sorts of parties, business parties, parties for the children, travel to the mountains, and an involved, fun-loving community that I was lucky enough to be a part of. People seemed happy and lived accordingly. It's not hard but not easy to point out such communities or neighbourhoods today. As new immigrants in a not-so-populated locality, times were straightforward, and life was good. I was a kid back then, so times were to be simple anyway. But the stories of children who have not had healthy lives early on are way too many, and so I cherish my roots deeply. Unfortunately, as the story goes on, you'd come to know that it is not just the children with unhealthy upbringings that get caught up in what society deems *terrible*. Still, even children who were raised right could find themselves in places no one could have imagined. I could not have imagined it if my younger self saw what would soon become of me. A life well lived only to reach points of violence and revenge, rage and despair.

I don't know what it was, perhaps a genetic factor; I was physically stronger than kids my age, even though I was one of the shortest in my class, giving me that Napoleon syndrome edge. I was athletic and determined. I did track and field, played soccer, and started playing football, my most liked sport in junior high. So yeah, I was strong but also fast, so I did pretty good as backup running-back to our starting running back, who was in his senior year. When *Kofi*, our starting running back, would go to college, I would finally get my opportunity to shine and show everyone around me how good I was, just after summer, which was around the corner. I had a knack for football, and many of the practices and games I attended would lead me to believe that I would capitalize on the opportunity to my utmost potential when the shift happened. But life had other plans.

But more on that later.

I wouldn't go ahead without mentioning my best friend from the past, Deon Foxford. He was half-Asian and European and quite an interesting character. Later, I found out the reason he took a liking to me, a reason that will stay between him and me for now. I do want to say that the common notion of how we *despise the ones who are too peculiar to us* is true, but often, we come closer to the ones who are the most peculiar to us as well. Deon was my best friend, and I owe a lot of my early joyful memories to him.

So when my father's business started soaring, we moved towards the suburbs, which entailed us buying a new suburban house and switching to the nearby school. A suburban house costs around 80,000 CAD; prices are now up to 6 times more. We were the only black family there as far as I can remember, even though our neighbor had a good mix of Indians, Chinese, Italians, and Americans apart from the locals.

So people from different cultures and backgrounds were situated together, and hence, groups of children our age mingled accordingly; there was no actual bias towards who to hang with and whatnot. People of different ethnicities enjoyed themselves together, and so did I, yet I had an innocent longing to meet with people of my color. Black people, as I hadn't seen many black people, if at all. A major reason why I was excited to go to high school and so I ended up going to *Harry Ainley High,* the biggest high school at the time in western Canada. The high school was divided in clicks, and everybody had a corner or a particular section, divided by race, religion, color, jocks, nerds, preps, and so on. I knew there I would find black people and get a chance to mingle with those whom I deemed a singularity. Fortunate are those who understand that we are all similar from within, no matter the visible differences among us; many spend their whole lives indulged in ignorance and secularity, division and separation, rather than the significance of the *oneness* of us all. But it intrigued me as a young black kid who had only seen a few black kids, or any for that matter. Most of the kids looked different to me, and for the less civilized, less socialized child, needless to say, the well-known saying of. *"Oh... Your hair is so curly!"* is one that comes to mind.

Interestingly enough, being an extroverted athletic kid, I also had an introverted side; I guess ambivert is the correct term. Which one would find hard to believe by looking at me, especially now as my appearance seems triggering. But I used to love comic books, and the addiction to reading them was real. I landed a job delivering newspapers to make money to feed the need to read. I worked hard so that I could afford comic books. I would take the newspaper ads and fliers, travelling with my wagon and distributing door to door. I was my father's son, and so the influence was visible.

On the other hand, my father had decent money but wasn't really flashy. I learned through him that secure men who know who they are and what they are capable of do not have traits such as cockiness and the need to show off. They taught me how to love myself and be a leader. Their validation comes from themselves and not others. They are indeed the living definition of being a *master of your fate.* They live how they want to live; they live for themselves and not how others want them to. A man who has achieved what he had set out to achieve has been validated and does not need the latest Ferrari to prove to the world otherwise.

So, my father's hard work laid the foundation for our success. But unfortunately, I was caught up in what would change the course of the rest of my life. I was about to be introduced to a whole new world, a world I wanted to be a part of, without knowing what it fully entailed. I was a young kid excited to meet new people without fully understanding or knowing what was out there. Out there in the wilderness, the sheer darkness that a child from a well-off family is usually unaware of. The darkness that parents fear their kids will fall into, a void that sucks the lives of human potentiality. A dark that appeals to our younger selves for some reasons. For me, that side of life was new and completely foreign. But also, as yin-yang indicates, there is a little bad in good and vice versa, including living beings, so the appeal to darkness exists in our nature, and I wasn't afraid of the dark. Needless to say, the next few years changed and molded me in a way that, even to this day, I take myself with me wherever I go.

2

Crossing Paths with a Gangster

Indeed all excellent pieces of literature are one of two stories; a man goes out on a journey, or a stranger comes to town. Overall, High school was quite an experience. I was going to school with my best friend, Bjorn. I remember how excited we were; it was a completely fresh experience. On our first day, we met and made two very good friends, Sam and Jomo. Finally, I had some black friends, and it was interesting to see how many looked like me but belonged to different cultures and spoke different languages; the diversity was magnifying. All were first-generation black guys who came from other cultures. Africans, Jamaicans, Asians, Trinidadians, to name a few; there were more. Interestingly enough, we all went to the same school and met each other for the first time, and the gathering felt comfortable; it felt right.

It wasn't just us; there was a pattern here. It was not long before the Asian kids, white kids, Lebanese, Middle Eastern and Indians had all gathered and met each other. They were happy to be around familiar faces, a feeling foreign to a special kind of people, the immigration kind. So everyone formed groups with others of similar color, culture, and race, but at the same time, they interacted with each other. Almost everyone I knew went along; we had the football players, the jocks, the basketball players and, of course, the cheerleaders. Anyway, lots of girls, interestingly enough, lots of Asian and East-Indian girls. We hung out with girls from all races and had a friendly experience, generally, Latinos, Indians, and Puerto Ricans. The Clueless Girls, a group we hung out with back in the day, were a mix of South American, Puerto Rican, Native American, Filipino, Iranian and French Canadians. Most kids with this opportunity of freedom had the time of their lives to be young and crazy. We used to go out, smoke weed, and just a bunch of crazy teenage stuff—one of the best times of my life.

However, these different groups of people, separated and individual, lead to confrontation. So there were groups of us black kids and other kids, and things would get rough. Some of us went to the same school, while other black kids knew or were mutual friends and lived around the same neighbourhood. Interestingly enough, due to cultural and religious values, the East Indians were specific about how their women should not date outside of their culture and, in particular, black guys. At the same time, their older brothers would be rather adamant about it. Anyway, all of them were generally open-minded people yet also close to their core values at the same time. That's the beauty of Canada: different people are sewn into one big group. Even regarding color, I remember the white guys with whom we had mutual respect and understanding. If a fight broke out, we had their back, and they had ours.

It was around grades 11 and 12 that the aspects of our teen life started to change. It was perhaps manhood, a realization of self-importance, or insecurities that would, in turn, cause confrontations amongst one another on the smallest of things. We'd go to parties as before, but now situations would escalate and get dangerous for the ones involved and the others around them. An argument over a black guy trying to date a brown woman. An argument between black and brown guys over track pants. It wasn't about the pants, but rather just feeling the mutual need to display masculinity. I can say this now, of course, but needless to say, back then, I was no saint either. I was trying to talk to a brown girl myself back in the day; her name was *Praveena*. Some of her brown relatives had found out and were not happy about it; they tried to retaliate. You know how it goes. This was really a common theme in why fights would break out, having vengeful agendas against each other on petty concerns.

It was about this time that we were at a party at this club called Caribbean Flavors. It was a pretty big party with quite a crowd. Anyway, someone said the N-word, and the next thing you know, a fight broke out. One of the guys that were involved was Usman Perez. He was an East Indian Muslim who belonged to a well-off family. He had a way with words; people were drawn to him. Many of the brown guys looked up to Usman and used to listen to everything he had to say. He wasn't your average street thug; he was well-read. He took his values and cultural principles seriously and had shades of his seniors in him; people liked him. He was about 16/17 in grade 11. Brown kids followed him quite a lot, so he was their leader. His sister had married a black guy, which her family did not like, and so there was an underlying feeling in Usman for the black community that was soon to boil to the surface.

But see, these brawls are never really a one-time thing. It goes on and on for as long as need be. A petty issue leads to a confrontation; someone gets slapped, punched in the face, or knocked cold into the shadow realm. Then we did something for fun called "Base," which happened at birthday parties. We would play amongst each other, get a few friends riled up with drinks and treat them to a good time while we beat them up throughout the night, giving them cheap jabs and thumps on the back, producing that base sound! But other than that, the street cycle was vicious. One guy gets jumped and beat up, goes to his friends, plans and executes his attack, a never-ending cycle, all for nothingness. However, a difference of significance here was that the brown kids came from richer backgrounds and, needless to say, had a circle of people around them. The black kids surrounding me weren't as rich; some were from good middle-class families and were doing well enough. Not all of them were, but certainly not like many brown kids at school. So we'd go to these parties where we did not have the fast cars, not the kind of money they had, but still enjoyed nevertheless. A lot of these black kids came from government housing, and so there was a significant contrast in the environments of the kids studying at the same school. Jomo and Sam were two of these black kids and my close friends. Jomo lived with his single mother, who worked hard to provide for her children, but because of her pursuit, she was not at home, and much so, in turn, got him the freedom to do whatever he wanted. On the other hand, I had my parents, worked a job and managed a car. So I'd get asked to attend these parties, regardless of the troubles, and join them for a good time.

One of the most dangerous facets of secularism is false prophets. We are our own people and should define ourselves rather than find ourselves; people in pursuit of finding themselves end up at the hands of false leaders. What makes a false leader is the low self-esteem of human nature, how it can decay into evil and give into personal agendas of hate to manipulate others for a sick feeling of satisfaction. Some kids, especially, are naïve and do not know any better. I can't sit here and write with certainty about why Usman wasn't fond of black people, or maybe it was just us. Frankly, I don't care. What I can say is that he did everything possible to manifest his hatred into reality. He used his charisma to charm people with strong words and a sense of confidence to get them to agree that he was right, that whatever it is needs to be done.

These confrontations had started to get serious, from jumping people with punches and kicks to now stabbing each other. It has become dangerous to step out of the house sometimes, especially if you have a target on your back. See, adults, they've learned, experienced, suffered, seen. Kids? They're new. They don't know, don't care and can be dangerous. Parties would turn into brawls, guys swinging fists, coming back, getting KO'd, madness. A good violent appetizer was the N-word; utter and shit hits the fence almost immediately.

A lot of these brown kids and Usman were from a different school, and so they would lurk around our school, predators, yet we were no different, beating each other up at the first opportunity seen. They'd come to our school, and we'd go to theirs. At this point, I wouldn't say I was involved in these pre-gang formations, but I was in it enough to speak. How the mind can be lured into toxic directions early on, but I was more focused on sports, yet I also knew what was going on between friends of my color and the others and had their back. What else do you do? Not help your brothers of color? As a young mind, that's what's right, and many of us live by that code until the end. Get into trouble for a brother in need. Some won't, claiming it to be a smart move, a lack of courage masked by fancy words. Responsibilities should not hinder us from keeping our and our loved one's self-respect. Standing for what is right for your people or whoever you associate with has been and will always be a courageous move. We all have our own sense of what's right and wrong.

At this point, a rivalry had begun between these kids, with Usman at one side. I know of him because he had made quite the name for himself, not different than the average cult mentality. Their self-made master was kept safe and surrounded. Guys who had jobs in shops and gas stations would have a target on their back because of their precise location and were attacked frequently; people would get stabbed, cars smash into each other, and physical confrontations had just become another aspect of life. Listen, you don't have to be involved in getting beat up; maybe you were seen with the Opps, or perhaps you were black and just so happened to walk past the wrong gang of brown boys, and vice versa. The predators would come at you like wolves on sheep. One guy gets beat at a mall, gets with his friends to maul any enemy who comes to hand, and then attacks one of the blacks, and it seemed as if this wasn't a loop that was ending anytime soon.

One of the leading guys from the black side was a good friend of mine, Jamie Battle, a loud-mouth big guy who played defensive line in football. People would often get into trouble because of him and his glorified attitude. Adrian and Phil were also my friends who were involved, at least much more than my friend Sam and I were at the time. Kids of our age all knew that a war was taking place, building, especially with the stories roaming around about the stabbing. A group of kids had broken into a house and stolen guns, and it turned out later that weaponry was sold to Usman. At the time, Usman was arrested for selling weed. He'd made quite a living and made good money selling it. Needless to say, drug dealers are popular amongst youth for obvious reasons. A drug supplier has power over addicts that no human being should have upon another. The power is, however, immense in volume. So, Usman was to be arrested and spend time in jail. It was then he came to our school to seek confrontation, and it just so happened that Jamie, the Jomo, and the Deons were not there. So, while they were here to seek trouble, those who would have loved to cater to them were not here. We were there, kids who weren't interested in whatever they were looking for. Simply put, they were looking for big black boys to mess around with. A couple of my friends and I were passing by them in the high school parking lot when the next thing you know, we had a gun pointed at us by Usman.

As I write, I reminisce and feel as if that was one of those moments in my life where I discovered more of myself than anything else. You'd imagine a good kid from a lovely family to back down to a strong thug, especially when having a gun pointed at my face, but no. These people were, after all, enemies of my friends. What friends? Brothers. Of course, having a gun pointed at your face is a feeling unique to the situation. But in front of all those people, what was he really going to do? Or so I thought and went with it. I blatantly called him a bitch to his face. That he would do nothing, and it was better to walk away. He did. It was one of those moments where everyone, including me, was somewhat surprised by how I stood up against Usman. Still, they also knew of another matter, and so did I. See, there's most certainly calmness before a storm, but sometimes there is a calm after it. Because of my courage? Partially. Partially because everyone knew what that storm pertained to.

I believe the motive behind this visit was that one of their members was stabbed. So they had access to a gun and so had to show off their newfound power. The fact that it did not go well for him, the dominance he wanted to accomplish, was what I thought could come back to bite me in the back. Someone bringing a gun to a high school was something unheard of in our peaceful neighborhood. It was almost unbelievable, and so much attention wasn't paid by any relevant authorities to the situation.

When I told the homies about what went down and that he may come after me, they didn't seem to think so. That even if he did, they would be there and handle it. They wanted a piece of Usman anyway. However, I had a feeling that something was about to happen. I had a really good feeling, so I spoke to the boys about having my back, which made me feel better about the situation. But for the most part, they didn't consider it as serious as I did, and that Usman was quite the bluff master. However, just before Usman had put his foot on the accelerator, we exchanged glances. The sadistic look in his eyes fed my instincts that something was, in fact, about to go down. At the time, I didn't feel that telling my parents would make the situation any better; I didn't think there was much they could do anyway. I had dared Usman to pull the trigger. I knew he could not. But the feeling that he might adhere to that dare sometime later, I was cautious.

Usman's family background wasn't much different than mine, a suburban kid whose parents owned a dollar store in the community. Usman worked the dollar store as a front job where his money and reputation would come from his drug-dealing activities. He was also in communication with people much older than him, like the older Southside cats, and would then use what he'd learned on the younger kids. Southside was the name of our click; we were all either from the Southwest or the Southeast but were all Southside. Southwest was smaller in comparison; Bjorn, Sam, Jomo, Mike, Tintin and myself were southwest. Southeast was Youks, Kofi, Sehan, Nigel, Phil, Jamie, Chad, Adrian, Yoofi, Steve, Chris, and Oketchie. Southeast is Millwood, a residential area in Edmonton, or as we called it, Illwoods. Most of it consisted of immigrants and is also where most trouble resided.

I pledge to my readers not to choose paths that have destinations you do not understand. Once you're there, it's too late. Or so it is, for most people. There are those who live to tell their story that they did, in fact, bounce back. In the latter, you've lost your freedom and will and given into weakness. Weed is alright, but back in the day, or even now, particularly for ill-advised kids, smoking a lot of weed can, in turn, become a dangerous enemy. Especially when the person providing it has ulterior motives and is much aware of the exchange you are bound to make with the devil. Human beings may seem different but are all too the same, and sometimes people use this understanding for manipulation. Know yourself and go out there and listen to what everyone has to say, research different sources, and then use your own individuality to compile an understanding of a certain matter. *Believe no one more than you believe yourself.* Cult mentality: following leaders and leaving your fate to another is unfair to the free will you possess as a human being. You have the right to practice your free will, do not waste it looking for saviors—men who tell you what to do with your life.

Try deciding for yourself; it's hard. It is hard but worth it. Do not let your guard down for someone who looks you in the eye and speaks with intent. Intentions and agendas are often cloaked by the essence of its sheer opposite. Learn to decipher the unspoken language of intention. Do not expect morality In return if you have the same to offer. Keep your eyes open and your mouth shut. Learn to observe and notice. Much like everything else, a habit can be unmade with constant repetitions, and you, too, will learn. Because why he said what he said is just as important as what he said.

3

Endgame

That same night, I remember telling my friends about it, but I seemed to be the only one bothered by a possible repercussion, so it wasn't taken as seriously by others in my group. The next day, the incident moved to the back of my mind, and I was less worried than I had been the day before. Anywho, it was about 1 o'clock the next day when I walked out of school with my boys towards the bus stop and noticed a car pulling up behind us. When the car pulled up, we were close to a nearby mall's parking lot. I noticed from a distance that a man got out of the car wearing a long trench coat, a baseball hat, and black shades. I had never seen this man before. He had gotten out of the passenger seat of the car and was pacing in on us. It was as if he was trying to catch up with us; I remember thinking that it was weird. We were a group, three homies and some girls, and the man was charging somewhat towards us as if he was going to attack, but that he could also not be, so it was open to interpretation. He seemed our age, 17-18, but the trench coat and shades in the summertime were what made it look suspicious.

By this time, almost all of my group had noticed the man walking in on us and discussing whether something should be done. We had a feeling that it could have something to do with Usman. But first, it didn't seem like Usman nor his car, and second, it was highly unlikely that the man would, for instance, take out a gun in broad daylight and shoot us in the face. This positivity or positive notion was what led to us not paying attention, and we didn't really consider it as a threat, let alone a deadly one. It was near when we decided to avoid it altogether, and then he started closing distance between us. Being the one who first noticed him, I looked back again and noticed the distance between us, seemingly shorter than before. That wasn't the only thing I noticed. He put his hand in his coat.

Maybe at that time, in that split second, I knew what he was going to take out. But one doesn't know until he knows. I knew when I saw the same gun that Usman had pointed at my face just yesterday now pointed at me, yet again. So we noticed it and began to run for our lives while the man chased us, me in particular. Screaming, though whatever his content was, I do not remember. Most of me not remembering has to do with what followed.

So yeah, we all ran in a different direction and as fast as we could, but I ran with more intent. We all knew who he was after. I was running towards the parking lot, hoping to get cover behind the parked cards. So I ran. I ran as fast as I could to the best of my ability. Knowing that if I stop, I will die. That this was it and that if I stopped, my life was over. The undercover getup and the gun were enough indication of how this was as real as it could be and wasn't just another mere scare-off.

Almost near the parking lot for cover, I glanced back at the guy pacing fast, who fired a shot again. I ran and focused my direction on a car nearby. If I could get some cover, I would regroup and see what I could have done. Maybe he wouldn't have noticed me hiding there; maybe I could have found another spot or perhaps redirected him one way or another. If only I could decide. If only I had reached where I wanted to. Maybe I could've run faster. A thousand times has, this story played in my mind. Because when I had almost reached the brink of the car, I suddenly dropped and skidded across the ground.

Shock is an interesting state of mind. Adrenaline numbs the senses no matter how heightened. What the hell just happened? I was running for my life, and then my leg gave out. My mind rushed to the conclusion that maybe I'd tripped and fell. I was unaware of what had happened yet fully aware of the man behind me. I turned back and noticed the man running up to me with the same .44 Calibre that was pointed at my face yesterday. He was screaming something at me as he ran up to me, dumping the shots in my direction and shooting me in my leg.

I was shot twice. Twice until the man decided to stand over me. The remaining bullets in the six-rounder were fired onto my helpless body. I couldn't move much but did what I could do to dodge the bullets as he fired them. He wasn't really quick about it. He took his time. He emptied the revolver onto me. While he was shooting me, I begged him to stop. To not kill me, that he did not have to do this. Yet he had not come only to stop now. I did not understand at that time how he was so motivated to commit to such a task, which really, for the most part, was nothing. It was for nothing. I was shot for nothing.

The discovery of the emptied revolver came about when he aimed the gun to my face. He fired; nothing. If he hadn't wasted his first bullet shooting aimlessly at the crowd, I would not be here writing my story. Or perhaps someone else would: a friend, a family member, a loved one. But amongst all this chaos was what seemed like a glimpse of something when I heard the empty click. My friends Sehan and Orin took cover behind a car nearby, noticed that the gun was empty and came after him with his pocket blade, but it was too late. The man took off.

I knew I was alive. I was shot repeatedly, but I was alive. I felt myself breathing heavily. Blood everywhere around me, legs that I just can't seem to feel. I couldn't feel my legs, nor could I feel the fact that I had just experienced myself getting shot. Where was the pain? I do not know. It was there, most certainly. But at the brink of such an abyss, when you understand the simple fact: You are about to die. What pain do you expect to feel?

I felt nothing but the fact that it was over. That life was over, that I'd made a mistake, and now I was to die. You only know what you have when you don't, and lying down bloody in the parking lot, I saw my life reel spin into play. My beautiful family, my friends, my life… 5 minutes ago. Hopefully, a time would come when my sister would get married, and when that time comes, I would not be there. Amongst this self-reflection, I didn't see myself; I saw my absence in the people who loved me. I cared about their feelings and realized it wasn't about me; it was about them.

During this time, while I was in survival mode consciously, all such thoughts passed through my subconscious as a train of many thoughts. Thoughts such as memories and faces. All the places I had to be, all the people that would be expecting me, in particular my house. They finding out that I wasn't coming home, and what that would be like for them. My mind had accepted defeat; I was lost in what could have been; I was lost in what I had. Maybe the whole life passing by in front of your eyes before death is shown only because it's not only the last time you'll feel something; it's the last time you'll experience what it's like to have a memory.

As I reminisce, like I have a thousand times before, I remember it all being so bright. A light, perhaps, that seemed to have gone brighter. Something that pulled me, or maybe I was compelled towards it. It's interesting because you don't understand this experience just as much as you do, understand. And so when it does happen, you let it occur. You go on with wherever you are being taken in this newly founded light. I knew what had happened and so went on with it as the light proceeded me further.

Fortunately, something held me back. The glimpses of my loved ones, my little sister, Dahlia, not being there for her as she grew up, got married, and had beautiful children. To see my parents grow older, to be there for them when they one day, after a long, healthy life, pass away. But I would not be there, and there would exist nothing but memories of me in the hearts of my loved ones, who would go on with life in my absence. This temporary regret wasn't long but seemed like an eternity. What pain was I to feel from some bullets in contrast to losing my loved ones forever? Looking back, it was the loud outburst of emotional pain and maybe some critical thinking that made me snap my head as my actual surroundings around me became somewhat vivid. I had felt what this light pertained to, and I wanted no part of it whatsoever. Lying there, partially paralyzed and bloodied up on the ground, mixed feelings of pain, fear, anxiety and anger summed up a silent victim shocked at what had just occurred.

I felt a tapping sensation on my face, and the blur slowly faded as I noticed my friend slapping me in my face, trying to get me back to reality, trying to get me to respond. I tried to open my eyes and focus, only to find faces in shock all around me. Not just my friends but a whole group of people had gathered around me. With all the questions coming my way while I was on the ground, needless to say, I had no idea how to respond. "Are you okay?" and "What do you want to do?" were delicate questions. I hesitated at," Should we call your parents?" In hindsight, yes, of course. But what was I supposed to say to them? I did not realize the seriousness of my condition and just asked the guys to get me out of there. I remember the spectators trying to call the police while I was trying to get them not to call, all the while trying to stay awake. I found out that some of the spectators had even tried to chase the shooter's car but were not successful. However, later that same day, the driver and the passenger were both caught.

When adrenaline dumps and reality kicks in, you realize you've been shot repeatedly. From all that it pertains to, the most evident feeling now was the physical pain. My friends tried to pick me up, but when they would try to move me, I'd feel pain, infinite and indifferent, than anything I'd ever felt. A girl from our group called my parents and told them to come there as soon as they could because their son had been shot. The girl was crying, and my mother had picked up the phone. As a man, I cannot imagine what a mother feels in such a situation. I would not compare it to the pain I felt that day. Physical pain is hindered, but emotional pain has no limitations.

I remember telling someone to call an ambulance and finding out they already had. I saw a nurse who came to me and tore off my clothes with a hospital knife to see where I was shot. It suddenly hit me. Man, I am not only shot but also naked, random in a mall's parking lot. Thank God for technology introducing itself when it did a bit earlier, and you'd probably see my naked ass all over YouTube, with subtle memes here and there.

I wasn't as calm as my writing may indicate. As you can imagine, I was terrified that I wouldn't be able to move again. The nurse did a good job of calming me down and also made use of my ripped clothes by wrapping them around the wounded areas. Nevertheless, the situation was handled well. Soon, the police arrived, and the nearby mall had been evacuated. I wasn't being questioned; the people around me were inquiring to find out what had taken place. The shot was heard, and there was a huge commodity in the parking lot. For those of you know, might wonder, how does one survive repeated shots from a .44 Calibre? Fortunately, these were buckshot buckets as opposed to real bullets. Buckshot bullets explode into different pieces, for better or worse, I did not know.

Apparently, I was lucky. I was indeed, as the nurse told me, I wasn't shot in the upper torso, head or heart but mainly in the legs and hip. All that body bobbing and weaving sort of saved my life. Soon came the ambulance, and I was taken. The Latina nurse was with me, and I kept asking her if I was going to die. I did not want to close my eyes and fall asleep, and as tempting as it was, God knows what it pertained to. Scared out of my mind, I told her that I did not want to die. I was all bloodied up, and so my condition was such that the nurse really couldn't say much. She tried her best to muster a smile that hid the answer to my question. She was lovely and comforted me by taking off her Rosary and putting it in my blood-soaked hand. She told me to hold on to it and to not lose faith. God knows how much of me sitting here and writing this book is because of her. I do not know your name, but I thank you from the bottom of my heart.

I remember reaching the hospital circled by a group of doctors and nurses looking at me using terminologies I had no clue of. A doctor asked me: How are you still alive? Well, I don't know. Am I? I did not want to sleep, but I felt the cousin of death tugging at me and showing me a light too bright to gaze at. At this point, the will to live had grown strong in me, and I found myself fighting to move, fighting to think, fighting to breathe, but the doctors wanted me to sleep, so they put a mask on my face and just like that I was out for three days.

Surgery had to be conducted, but none of these doctors or medical students at the hospital had dealt with gunshot victims before, let alone multiple shots. Apparently, a specialist from the U.S. was here training them on conducting and dealing with unique gunshot surgeries, and me being the pioneer of gunshot tragedies in Canada, the party soon began. They cut open like a butcher in a meat shop, taking out the bullets and cleaning up the wounds. Since the bullets were buckshot and had exploded, there were traces of shrapnel in my hip that could be spread all over my body. Correction: there are shrapnels in my hip even to this day, 25 years after the incident. Something so serious should have been dealt with when I got the opportunity post-recovery, but I did not. Youngblood gets revenge, but let's save that for later.

After some days post-surgery, I woke up only to notice an array of tubes and wires attached to me, with something in my mouth that prohibited my speech. I tried to talk, but I couldn't; I realized that I wasn't able to move most of my body; even breathing brought agony. I had immediate surgery, and the doctors had ripped me open. I was told that my body was inflamed and so much of me had bloated up. This pretty face of mine couldn't even be noticed anymore. I knew what had happened to me, and waking up to a version of me that could not talk, move and breathe properly while a dozen tubes were attached to me brought upon a feeling I'd never wish on an enemy. I wanted to move, get up, talk, and go back home. But I was confronted with the fact that the last memory I had of my healthy self was running aw

I cannot forget the look

need adjectives or verbs, no

speak or move. I was given

I write? I wrote, "Mom, I w

of relief and joy that her bo

writer good enough to desc

I was told to press a but

my father and my sister cam

school, the biggest in weste

and the incident was reporte

affection I received from th

societies and cultures have

different. Canada was, and s

and the reflection showed i

times without asking nor ex

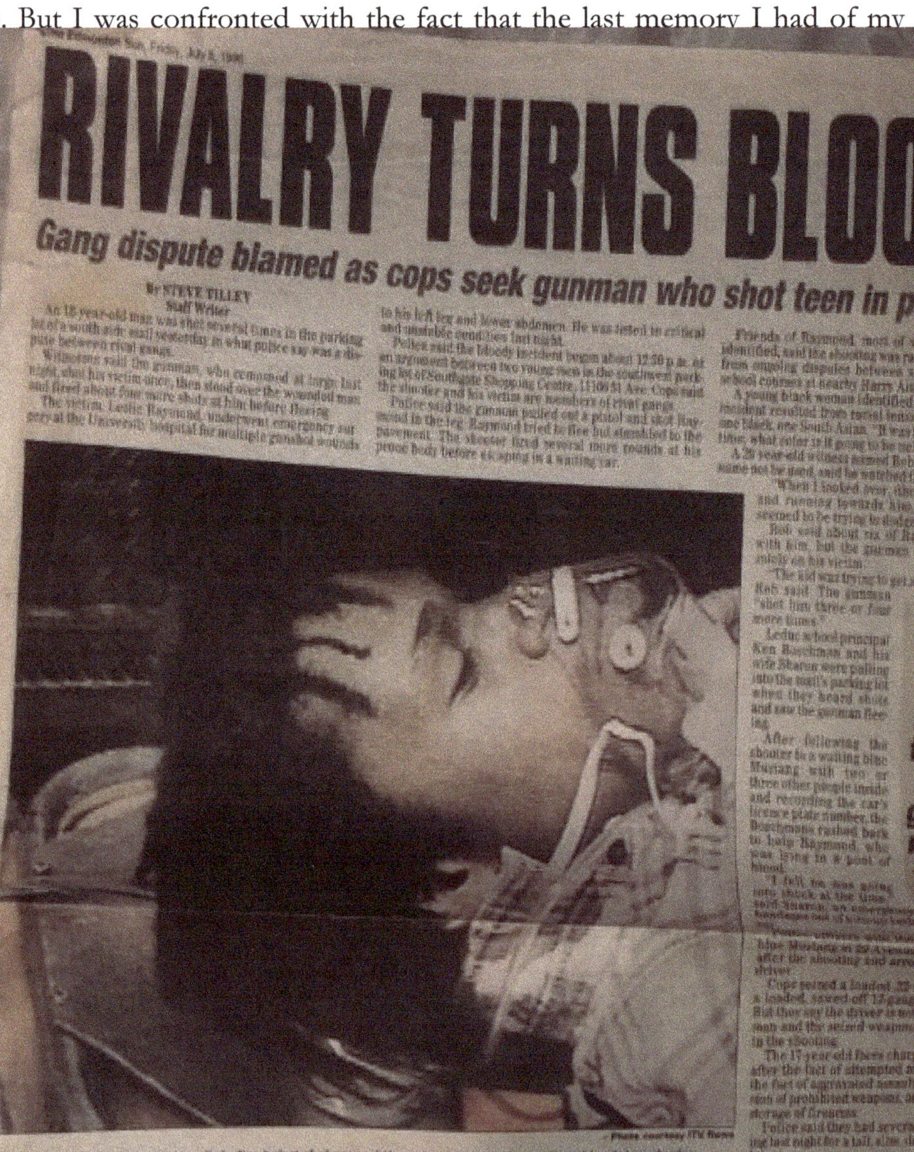

RIVALRY TURNS BLOOD

Gang dispute blamed as cops seek gunman who shot teen in parking

By STEVE TILLEY
Staff Writer

An 18-year-old man was shot several times in the parking lot of a south side mall yesterday in what police say was a dispute between rival gangs.

Witnesses said the gunman, who remained at large last night, shot his victim once, then stood over the wounded man and fired about four more shots at him before fleeing.

The victim, Leslie Raymond, underwent emergency surgery at the University hospital for multiple gunshot wounds to his left leg and lower abdomen. He was listed in critical and unstable condition last night.

Police said the bloody incident began about 12:30 p.m. at an argument between two young men in the southwest parking lot of Southgate Shopping Centre, 11100 51 Ave. Cops said the shooter and his victim are members of rival gangs.

Police said the gunman pulled out a pistol and shot Raymond in the leg. Raymond tried to flee but stumbled to the pavement. The shooter fired several more rounds at his prone body before escaping in a waiting car.

Friends of Raymond, most of whom didn't want identified, said the shooting was race-related and from ongoing disputes between students taking school courses at nearby Harry Ainlay high school.

A young black woman identified only as Monica said the incident resulted from racial tension between two gangs, one black, one South Asian. "It was brown against black one time, what color is it going to be next time," she said.

A 20-year-old witness named Bob, who asked that his name not be used, said he watched the shooting in disbelief.

"When I looked over, the gunman was on him and running towards him," Bob said. Raymond seemed to be trying to dodge the bullets.

Bob said about six of Raymond's friends were with him, but the gunman seemed to be solely on his victim.

"The kid was trying to get away, but he fell," Bob said. The gunman "shot him three or four more times."

Leduc school principal Ken Boschman and his wife Sharon were pulling into the mall's parking lot when they heard shots and saw the gunman fleeing.

After following the shooter to a waiting blue Mustang with two or three other people inside and recording the car's license plate number, the Boschmans rushed back to help Raymond, who was lying in a pool of blood.

"I felt no use going into shock at the time," Sharon said.

Cops seized a loaded .22 caliber and a loaded, sawed-off 12 gauge shotgun. But they say the driver is not believed to be the gunman and the seized weapons weren't the ones used in the shooting.

The 18-year-old faces charges including accessory after the fact of attempted murder, accessory after the fact of aggravated assault, two counts each of prohibited weapons, and two counts of storage of firearms.

Police said they had several leads and were searching last night for a tall, slim, dark-skinned male late teens.

Leslie Raymond is taken to hospital after being shot several times in the Southgate mall parking lot yesterday.

span of a short week, a great population of the nation of Canada found out what had occurred in the parking lot of a small neighborhood in Edmonton, Alberta.

Shot teen feeling 'like I'm Superman'

JAMES STEVENSON
Journal Staff Writer

Edmonton

One week after being shot three times at close range in a parking lot, 18-year-old Leslie Raymond is still astounded by his good fortune.

"I feel like I'm Superman — sometimes bullets go through me," Raymond said Thursday, despite wincing in pain at the slightest movement.

The teen has undergone surgery twice since bullets tore through him, leaving six holes — entry and exit wounds — in his legs and stomach area. He has a large incision stretching down his stomach and expects to have at least one more operation.

Raymond said he knew the 17-year-old accused of pulling the trigger as "an acquaintance" at Harry Ainlay high school, but doesn't know why he was singled out.

Nor does he know why the shooter stood over him and shot him twice more after hitting him once in the leg.

"Maybe he went trigger-crazy or gun-happy."

Raymond was walking with six friends across the parking lot of Southgate shopping centre on July 4 when they saw a teen walking down the street by himself. Suddenly the teen pulled a gun, and the group scattered, said Raymond. Raymond was then shot.

The pain of his injuries didn't register until he was in the ambulance on the way to the hospital. But the fear started immediately. "It's so scary, you don't know what you're going to do — keep going or just give up."

But Raymond, a slotback on the school's high school football team and a keen Edmonton Eskimos fan, didn't die. He says he didn't want to be known as someone who gave up on life.

The teen initially thought he'd be in hospital for years, then months, and now doctors say he could be out in about three weeks. He's confident that he will be able to walk again and recover from his injuries.

He says only time will tell if the shooting leaves him with residual fear and rage, but he already is plagued by terrible nightmares of the ordeal. And despite not being religious, he believes that God had a hand in keeping him alive.

Two 17-year-old youths appeared in court this week charged with attempted murder, aggravated assault and various weapons charges. They plan to fight their automatic transfer to adult court.

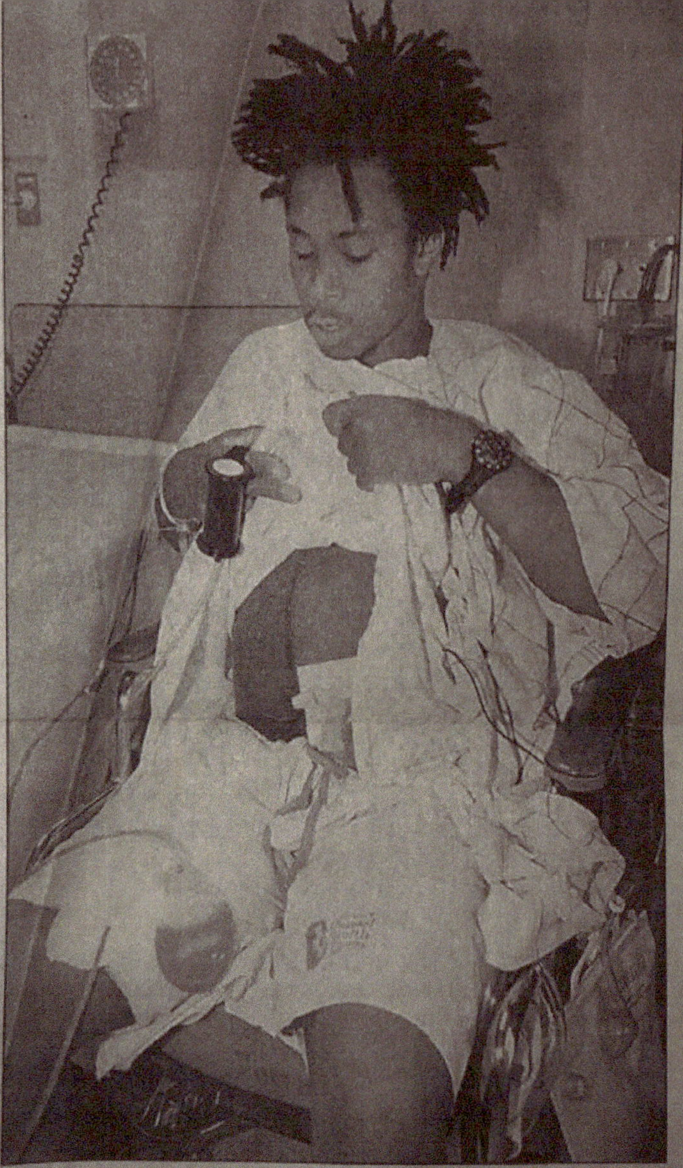

Ed Kaiser, *The Journal*

Leslie Raymond shows the scar from his life-threatening ordeal

Oil well drilling

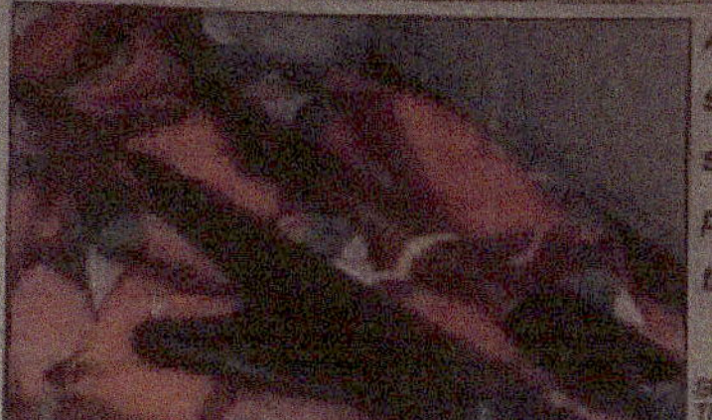

Gang feud cited in Southgate shooting

Gunned down

...AMS
Staff Writer

Edmonton

18-year-old Leslie Raymond writhed in pain, his young attacker stood over him and more bullets into his body — the end a power struggle between two racial police say.

...man, described by police as 18 to 20 and dark-skinned, fled in a car.

...earlier a group of black friends ...mer school at nearby Harry Ainlay ...ol were walking across the South... parking lot just after noon Thurs... a man began firing a handgun into...

"... shooting while he was running," ...ess Marcee Johnson, visiting here ...into ...e group of students scattered when shots rang out.

...heard at least four shots but police ...many as six bullets were fired.

Raymond's friends said he was not ...t by the gunman, but tripped as he ...

...believe Raymond and the gunman ... other, said police information offi... ...e Bidniak.

...ey have been involved in an ongo... ...e."

...ooting was the result of a power ...etween two rival racial groups ...de up of students from Harry Ain... ...d.

...ups "are punks and they're fighting ... You can call them gangs although ...no colors. They're kids who hang ...r."

... Sharon Boschman from Leduc ...ng into a parking spot at Southgate ...heard the shots and saw the gun... ...ng towards their car.

...ught about following him on foot ...cided to follow in their car.

Please see SHOOTING/A20
Back page of this section

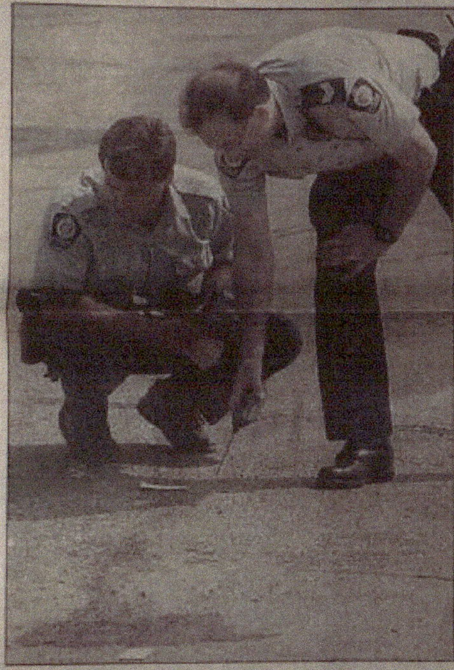

Greg Southam, The Journal
Police inspecting the scene after the victim was taken to hospital

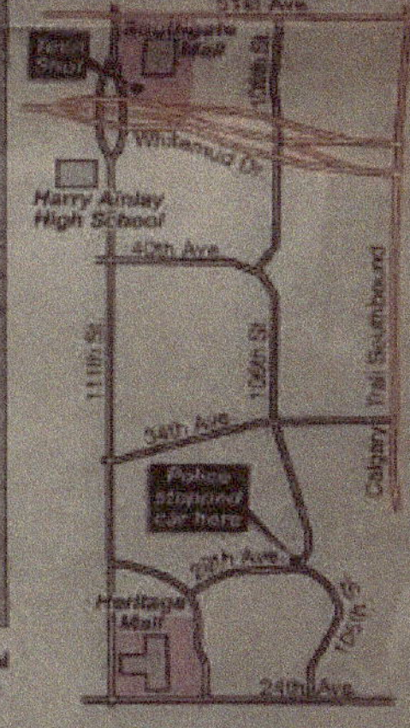

Fearful vigil for shot teen's parents

...OMSON
...Writer

Edmonton

...nutes of learning their ...had been shot, Sheila ...Raymond sat fidgeting ...out-of-the-way nurses' ...University Hospital's ...department.

...know anything," said ...cing through the open ...someone would come ...her son. "We were told ...cious but we haven't ...doctors."

...nd sat quietly across ...ead bowed, shoulders ...ds draped on his lap.

"He is good kid and a hard worker," Sheila said.

They are proud of their 18-year-old son who was born in Edmonton after they moved here from the West Indies island nation of St. Lucia.

He is taking math at summer school in the mornings. In the afternoon and evenings he works part-time at two McDonald's restaurants earning spending money. In the fall, planned to go back to Harry Ainlay school to finish Grade 12.

Sheila perked up after learning police at first considered her son's condition "non-life threatening."

But almost immediately a nurse ran into the room and said, "You have to come, now!"

"Is he all right?" asked Sheila.

"No," said the nurse, reaching for Sheila's hand and almost pulling her to her feet. "You'd better come now."

Leslie had suffered a cardiac arrest.

He was rushed to the operating room. Staff let the parents get a glimpse of their son as they wheeled him away.

Sheila's sobs followed her son's gurney down the hall and she had to be led back into the nurses' room by her husband, who closed the door.

A short while later the halls were clogged with friends and family joining in the agonizing wait.

Just about everyone described Leslie as a great guy and plenty of fun.

"He's by far one of our best employees," said Enid Dufresne, manager of the 23rd Avenue McDonald's where Leslie worked two or three shifts a week.

"He was a happy-go-lucky guy and great with kids."

He also worked at the McDonald's at Heritage mall.

"He was always real polite, a nice guy," said Jon Stringham, 18, who had a locker next to Leslie's.

His friends described him as someone who was always laughing, "like a child at heart."

Gang violence ends in 18-year-old going down in hail of gunfire: Page

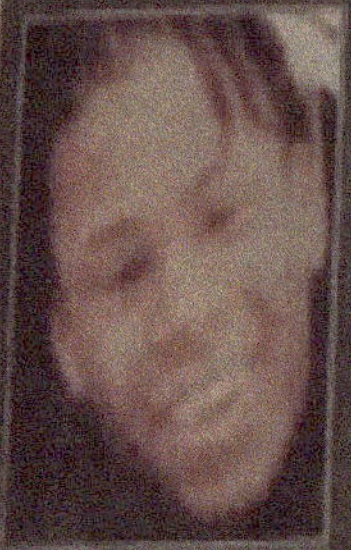

TEEN SHOT AT MALL

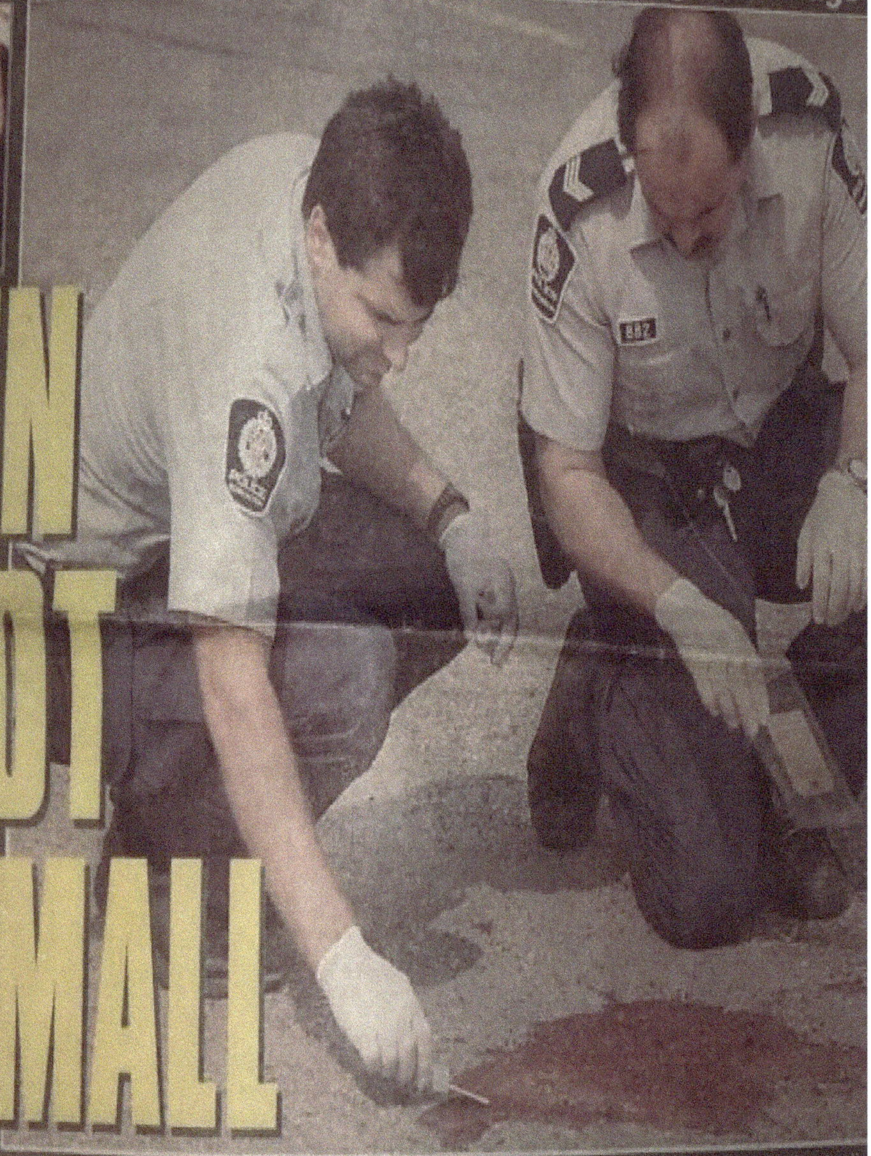

City police take a sample of blood from the shooting scene at Southgate Shopping Centre yesterday. Leslie mond (above left) is in critical condition in hospital with several gunshot wounds.

4

Everything, Nothing, Something

Dreams. When you're in them, you often come to the realization that, hey, wait. All the crazy shit that's happening, it's got to be a dream. There's that, and there's another type of dream, one you wish for. One you wish that it was, in fact, a dream. I thought I was dreaming too, until I found it was real. It was all real.

The mental state I was in is hard to explain, mostly because it was a combination of different emotions that left me in a complete state of shock. I couldn't feel most of my body, and all I could think about was the fact that my life was over. The fact that whoever I was, I wasn't and couldn't be anymore. Both my parents showed incredible strength in handling the situation, and I am proud. Some of my friends, on the other hand, would weep after looking at my condition. It was these little moments that made me realize the devastation of the whole situation. To see your loved ones look at you and succumb to the sheer visual of your condition is just as devastating for the person going through it. To see your condition but in the eyes of others. To see their eyes take drift when they look at you, the change in demeanour when they glance towards you, especially for the first time. To constantly be reminded of your situation in the reflection of the eyes of all who come across you. As if my physical and mental situation wasn't enough for me to feel the depths of my situation. But that wasn't all.

See, I was a specimen. In particular, I would like to thank the medical students and new doctors who would come by to examine me and learn more about the medical side of such incidents. I was one of the first gunshot victims in my province, Alberta, and so my case was unique for the time and of interest to many medical representatives. At the time, I found it to be quite cool. Every day, I was on display for someone where my bandages would be taken off, and a doctor would literally put his fingers inside my wounds and flip me to the other side to assess further, which wasn't fun, particularly because of the pain I used to go through. The rarity of my condition brought on a lot of constant observation, not just from the doctors assigned but all the other young and experienced aspiring doctors. They would observe and pass comments amongst themselves, it's all I saw for a good portion of my time there. I used to either wake up in pain or wake up in pain. The pain wasn't a feeling anymore that I'd feel every now and then like a normal person. The pain was my routine.

There were factors that I could have taken motivation from, but the abundance of my suffering weighed more than anything else. They had told me the seriousness of how close I was to death. I had cardiac arrest; one artery was tied to another, and at one point, they had to bring me back. I don't even remember the last bit. I was proud of the fact that when I was being shot at, I was bobbing, and weaving had literally saved my life. The doctors told me that even though the attack was severe, no major organs were damaged. I imagine a lot of people would have frozen for one reason or another, but I was an athletic kid and managed to well save my life.

The major complication was due to the shrapnel, which I have been dealing with to this day. Apart from the loss of blood, shrapnel had spread in major parts of my body, from my groin all the way to my back, as well as the heart. Even after I got out of the hospital, there was shrapnel in my heart that stayed with me for quite some time until my body finally flushed it out. As I am writing this chapter, I still have a surgery I need to tend to. There's a big chunk of a bullet on my right butt cheek that has grown into a giant-sized tennis ball. It's rather uncomfortable, and due to COVID, the surgery is getting delayed. Something I've got to tend to soon enough.

I was there in the hospital for some time, and after a while, loneliness began to creep in. Not that I was completely alone, friends, family and so many other people came by, but it was those little moments. How you feel when you are alone depends on your demons. My demons represented utter devastation. At night, I could hear machines being moved about and the sounds of chitter-chatter of the nurses, but that was all. I did not want to be alone; you reflect when you're alone. I did not want to, but I had to. Because I was no longer who I was some days ago. Man, I wished I was that kid from some days ago.

Fear lurked in the confines of my subconscious, thinking that something more could happen. At first, they had security guards outside my door, which changed when the situation started to settle. It didn't settle with me, of course, because, in my mind, it wasn't over. Perhaps it wasn't? Someone could walk through that door right now and kill me. Someone could walk through that door and finish what they started. The spiral of negative thoughts is a serious curse; it starts with a seed and then just grows, especially when watered. Even long after I was out and about, parking lots got to me. On July 4th, on a beautiful summer's day at 2 pm, I was shot in broad daylight surrounded by many people, like it was a typical day. The fact that it could just as easily happen again, anytime, was a real possibility in my mind. Even if I knew for a fact I wasn't to be attacked again, that fear would not have left anytime soon. Scents, sounds, and locations are great examples of becoming anchors to a memory in my mind. Parking lots were my anchor, and they terrified me.

The doctors had to take out some of my veins from other parts of my body to tie up the holes in other parts filled with shrapnel, so they had to clean it from the inside. There was a big gaping hole in my leg, and every morning, they would change the bandages. I could see them take a long gauze out of my body. Then, they'd change the colostomy bag and pull out my catheter. This is why even on days I didn't wake up in pain, I still had to go through this painful regime. I remember seeing the look of accomplishment on the doctor's faces after these sessions. They did a pretty decent job, not that I have other experiences to compare it to, but considering the condition I was in, the version of myself I am today, it is truly remarkable. The colostomy bag was used as the shrapnel was inside my body and, in particular, the abdominal region, so they had to remove my asshole and reposition it outside of my body. I would watch this asshole muscle squeeze poop out into a clear bag that was attached to my stomach. This went on for three months while the insides of my stomach were healing. Then I had to go for another surgery for my asshole to go back where it belonged. I could have used medical terms to explain the situation but two things; one, it'd be less fun, and two, I want my readers to see all the shit that can happen to you on a bad day. Think twice the next time you're about to make a decision that can harm you in any shape or form. You may even be taught being at the wrong place at the wrong time. Trust me, you don't want to see your asshole outside of your body squeezing poop out. It is a sight rare to a few of us, an experience I would not recommend.

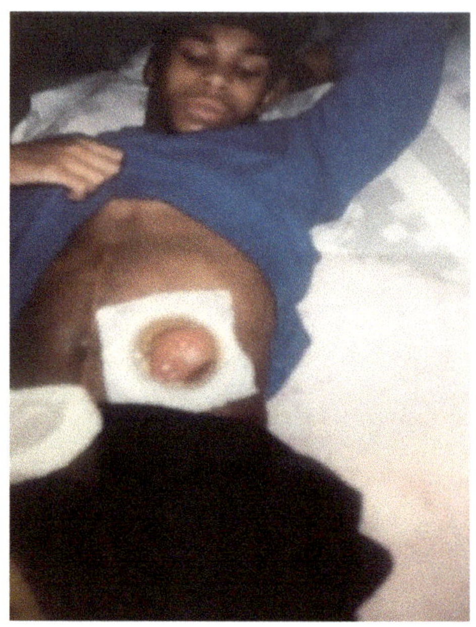

I had lost a lot of weight during this time and barely ate anything. When the doctors would visit for an early morning assessment, I would then have breakfast. I didn't eat much, I couldn't. This healthy 140-pounder kid had about 70 pounds left in him and little to no hope for a better future. All the future meant for me was that I would be attacked. What I had with me to tackle such thoughts was an abundance of love and affection. I would get mail, letters, flowers, postcards, and many gifts from not just my people but people from across the country. The news went viral for a good week, and so people who saw the news empathized and showed great affection through these little deeds, which did an awful lot for my mental well-being. It was because of this that I learned at a very early age that if there is bad, there is good. I was surrounded by it immeasurably to the point where they'd literally had to send people to recycle the stuff I was constantly receiving. To anyone who is reading and helped me during that time, I thank you.

Remember that button I was supposed to press for a dose of morphine? I was told to use it whenever I was in pain. The only problem here was I was in pain most of the time. So I pressed the living shit out of that button, and needless to say, I was flying high for most of the time. So many people used to come to me for blessings, and I'd be in my bed on a trip. This led to a point where I was told to calm down as I could get addicted to it if used often. It did make things fun, though.

I'd found out that the person responsible had been jailed. Turned out it was some wanna-be kid that got paid probably about $200 and a bag of drugs to do the job. His whole life went down the drain when he made that decision, all because he wanted to impress the man. Usman had such a strong influence over these people that they would literally do anything for him to attain his trust, to better their relationship and to progress further in his hierarchy. He never had to get his hands dirty, and his manipulative words were strong enough for his beta-wolves to cater to whatever their master said. I remember the man chasing me and reminiscing about my expectation that it should have been Usman coming after me. After all, I had pissed him off. Who was this stranger I remember going to school with once upon a time, trying to take my life? What could I have done to him that he came at me the way he did? As time passed, I realized it was all because that guy wanted to get ahead, and this was the right opportunity for him to step ahead, take responsibility, and meet his cult master's expectations. I feel for how that man wasted his life over a bad decision. All I can say is, don't be that person. Morality is what keeps a person in one piece. Don't break into the pressure of societal factors; don't stain your character for another. Integrity is a trait for few, but perhaps the most valuable virtue of them all.

From all that was going on in my head, what kept popping up was the fact that something was to happen. My friends would tell me how big this was and that if they were to do something about it, they had to retaliate. Even though an obvious part of me wanted retaliation, a part of me also knew that I could not feel half of my body. That I could possibly not walk again, never get a hard-on and that my education was over. I did not want the same for my friends, so I told them to stay away and not do anything about it, to let bygones be bygones. They laughed it off, saying I was high and that they would do something about it like there wasn't any other option. We were on different sides of the same spectrum.

I noticed how life was to continue as it was before but without me. The football team made the changes they had to make, classes I attended went on, and even the girl I liked had relocated. This realization really got to me that I would remain and would continue to remain in the same place, and everyone around me would move on. This was it for me. Back in the day, there were no psychiatrists and mental health doctors who would sit and talk to you. There was no focus on mental being especially not like how it is now. You were supposed to suck it up and deal with it, no matter how worse the situation was. I was surrounded by a lot of affection, but not everyone is, and I feel for those who had to go through such times with little to no support. The need to live no longer suffices; one could easily want to end it right then and there. I was a strong kid and never really considered giving up on life, of course, the support I had played a huge factor in me dealing with my situation the best I could. However, it's remarkable to see how much pain, agony, and sheer diversity a human being can deal with and still come out on top. We give ourselves little to no credit for the innate capabilities we all have. Indeed, we can do and go through much more than we think we can. We are what we believe in and more.

After a while, physiotherapy began, but it did not start well. Each time I tried to move as little as my toe, I'd fail and then continue on to drown in my sorrow. Each day, I had to try to get my body working again, but I kept failing. It was disappointing to keep failing while keep being reminded of what my future was to look like. I was in pain each time I tried, and a part of me did not want to do it. Too much had happened, and based on the past few months, my life was clearly not anywhere close to who I used to be. I did not want to make the continuous effort of trying to do something that wouldn't happen, and would in turn just bring me a world of pain. Every day, I had these painful sessions that I wanted no part of. *Why try? Why? Look at me. There's nothing left to save.*

But, of course, dusk follows dawn. It was just another day at the hospital, and I was in my wheelchair when another one pulled right next to me. We were schoolmates, a white kid, and quite popular at school. I was surprised to see him there and shocked to see someone like him in a wheelchair. He played hockey in high school and was quite the athletic one himself. Intrigued, I asked him what had happened. He then told me his story. Turned out he'd gotten drunk one night with his high school buddies near the train tracks where a train was to pass by. Young boys were drunk, messing around the tracks, and decided to jump onto the moving train cart. So one thing led to another, and the moving train ran over this kid's leg, who had slipped under the train while it was passing by and completely slicing his leg in half. It was devastating to hear that this kid seemed to have everything in school and was now sitting next to me in a wheelchair, missing a whole leg. I told him I was sorry for what had happened to him. His response played a significant role in where I was to go and from where I was.

Nothing serious; he just told me this. *Don't feel sorry for me. I did this to myself.* I felt him. Is that what had happened to me, or was I at the hand of another, but where he was, he put himself there? That it was no one but his fault, and so there was no one but him to blame. I couldn't help but think about it; young Les had never thought about it that way. At that time, I felt that the person in front of me had much more pain than I did. All this time, my focus was on myself and not around me. This was when I really began to realize empathy. I looked around, and I was not alone.

There was another lady who came in unconscious, on a stretcher, burned from head to toe. I've never seen a living human being in such a condition. Then there was another patient, a serious street assault. This black guy had apparently spoken to an Asian guy's girlfriend, who had literally beaten him to a pulp. He was brain-dead. This guy's whole life got ruined for something so silly that it killed me. I've been there, and I know how it feels to have a significant part of your lifetime wasted away all because of nothing. This guy literally lost his whole life. All such circumstances that I was surrounded with brought me to the realization that I had to do something. The realization that I was wrong. It was not over for me. If it was, then what about these people who had no chance at normality ever? I felt the need to act for me, just as much for my high school friend and others at the hospital whose journey continued but had reached an unfortunate destination.

So I gave it my all. We had a daily routine, and I took part to the best of my abilities. It wasn't long before I was able to move a toe. It was then evident to me that the process was working. Slowly and gradually, I had to learn to walk again. It was embarrassing, though, being a grown man learning to walk all over again. But all that had happened, I dealt with it. The process was excruciating as my legs were still in shock. I used to learn to walk in support of rails, and I remember my sister standing on the other end, motivating me to walk to her like a baby boy. My sister and my parents were there for me the whole three months I was there in the hospital, and I could never thank you guys enough. I love you.

After a good 12 weeks of pain and suffering, after what seemed like a dead-end, I found light and pursued it the first chance I got. I understood early on, because of this experience, the significance of empathy and how it teaches you to learn from the pain of others, to look outside of opinions and perspectives, and to be thankful for what you have. I went through hell and back, still living to tell the story. Maybe your pain is more than mine, maybe it's not. The point is that solace can be found, but we have to get out of our heads. Christianity, Judaism, and Islam, all accounting for more than half of the world's population, are belief systems based on the fact that the essence and meaning of life is simply living for others. To understand your pain, you must understand another's, hence the reason for writing this book. There is pain out there beyond your imagination and beyond your personal dilemmas, and while you might not care to pay attention to others, understand that tranquillity and harmony are not for a narcissist but for an empath. There is utter wisdom in the suffering of others; it is a rarity that unites us with all the good things in our lives, and it makes us appreciate all the good that is around us. Positive and thankfulness go hand in hand. Certainly, one does not work without the other.

5

Stairway to Solace

A lifetime of three months passed, and I was on my way home in a wheelchair. Things had started to get better. However, this is no indication of me seeking the bright lights ahead, as a good portion of me was still in utter despair. Yet I did enjoy how popular I and my case had become; different stories and rumours circled the city as to what had taken place. Different perspectives on the situation were being written in newspapers and articles; some of them were fake, yet I understood how the media and conspiracy work and understood the concept of publishing different interpretations and comprehensions of a particular situation.

But that was not all that was talked about.

In my time in the hospital, I was least interested in what the gang scene was like. With time, I learned that the people who put me in this position had grown in power. Though I did not pay that much attention, it was still in the back of my mind. The fact that they were still doing what they did and had now grown in numbers and reputation. The gangs were going at each other, as young kids were dying on both sides; a shit-show that I could care less about. Or so I like to think.

Because of my disabilities, the whole house situation had to change. I am sure we've all been in a situation where you're really grateful, yet a sense of guilt eats you away. The family that had been there for me through all this time, everything from routine to day-to-day household operations, had to sort of revolve around me. I had nerve damage on my feet and so could not even wear slippers. Then, there was my colonoscopy bag, which was there with me for another three months. Simple tasks such as sleeping in particular positions, like on my stomach, brought pain that would wake me up a bunch of times throughout the night. Yet so many people came to visit that I always had company, as supposed to be sitting with nothing but my agony to be depressed about.

The reason I said *a lifetime of three months is because those three months were the longest, to the point where,* for me, that place was the new home. Though I had grown to adapt to the hospital, the time I spent with my thoughts and the incident brought me obvious pain. See, home represented the past—the past before the incident. Going back home was a reference to some sort of normalcy, one that I had longed for the past three months, or at least the days I knew that I would be, in fact, one day, going home.

So, due to my condition, a lot had changed at home, as well as outside of it. Praveena had left just before the incident that had taken place, as well as certain situations with my friends as they continued on with the journey of life, and I had somewhat stopped in time. Also, coming back home, in a way, offered a different perspective of my own pain. Just like anyone else, home was a place where I came to spend time with my family, do homework, eat, and sleep, all the while living a life outside of it. But now, I am back at the same home, but not in the same life. This time around, everyone had to take care of me as I couldn't even walk or go outside for much of anything. In one way and just one, my time in the hospital could be considered better on the basis of, well… It was just a different life altogether. The surroundings did not remind me of the life I once had, at least not as much as my own bedroom did.

When it came to my future, there was nothing but uncertainty. When I think about my past and my future, I have a million feelings, one completely different from the other. The small-time gang scene was a big part of these kids 'lives, and you didn't know who you could trust. Like many of us, my family was the only people I could fully count on, more than anyone else. My childhood friend Bjorn, who had moved in with my family, soon had to move out due to a lack of security; living with me could possibly lead him to have a target on his back. Praveena had moved on with her life and is now married; it was sad for me to see everybody grow up and change. However, we still kept in touch via mail. But other than that, for the most part, it was just my family and me trying to make it through the many thoughts drifting through our minds. Any and all possibilities of the future I had visited every single one of them in my mind, Not knowing which one lay ahead.

On the contrary to what the news said, a lot of people thought the reason I was shot was because of an Indian girl or an even crazier one was track pants! Yet this was just another of the many stories that had gradually become nothing but white noise for me. Because of all the possibilities that were in front of me, I could not help but think about one, in particular, one where my life had resumed back to normality. I wanted to get better, and staying at the house also came with the realization that perhaps it was not over. I had gotten much better than how I initially was, and so there was no reason to stop.

I want to thank not just my incredible family but also my friends, who showed great patience and support towards me and helped me get better in any way they could. I could not have asked for more. Slowly but surely, in about three months of time, I was much better than when I first came home, which would never have been possible if I wasn't surrounded by the people I was. The people in your surroundings have a say in your sheer definition just as much as you do.

But friends, especially young friends, more so black young friends involved in the streets, can't let something like this go away. To be honest, I imagine no one would accept another bringing such a circumstance over a loved one. That's how gangs operate around the world; dominance and respect are what ensure successful operations. My friends were still going back and forth with Usman's gang. They wanted revenge. I'd be lying if I said I didn't want that. They had all these ways they could go about it, and even though I'd often give it thought, I didn't want to. Listen, a few months ago, I couldn't even feel half my body while I was dealing with the acceptance of perhaps never being able to walk again. The fact that I was getting better, more than anything, I was in a place of thankfulness. I was happy that my health was improving; I was happy to see that I most certainly could resume back to some sort of normality. Now, because I had another chance at life, what does a man do?

Roll the dice of life or gamble, never again?

I chose not to. Like a sane man would. Or like a man who had somewhat lost and didn't want to again. But that didn't last for long. Alas, we are all slaves to our sheer nature. As human beings, God's mightiest creatures, we don't want to lose. No one does.

At that point, I just wanted to move on. Ever since my accident, my routine mostly consisted of sleeping, playing games, hanging out with friends and family, and…. Well, that's most of it. My school was also supportive and really wanted me to come back and resume my education. The principal was obviously aware of what the kids had been up to and showed an interest in me talking to other kids about what happened, basically for awareness and to help them make better decisions. All the while, I solely focused on getting better, one day at a time.

A good six months after I came home, I was healthy enough to rejoin school. Even though I was behind on schedule and had to take some courses and overall just make up for the time lost, words cannot describe how happy I was to be back. To not just see the school but also getting to be a part of it meant everything to me. These were days I never thought I'd have again. But I did.

Needless to say, it was not all sunshine and rainbows. I couldn't play any sports at all, let alone play football. This was the year I was to play, but life had other plans. I would go to school on crutches and was also able to drive by myself. I had a plastic cast on my leg for support. Yet these circumstances weighed nothing against the fact that I was here with everyone else. The students made my journey a whole lot easier, and everyone helped out when they could.

So I went on, each and every day, with great support and a lot of determination to keep on getting better and going forward. My progress was my greatest motivator, as it should be for all of us. You stick to something and keep at it; results are not far away. What you can't do is stop. I did not, and while you may or may not have people around you who want to see you win, ultimately, it is in your own hands. For many, nothing is more terrifying than the uncertainty of the future. Many have succumbed to uncertainty, which often drives people to a lack of motivation, fear, and even depression. Patience and planning are your two best friends when it comes to facing what the future holds for you. For a while, I did not know if I'd ever be able to do anything at all; hell, I didn't even know if I'd live. I wanted to, but perhaps it was too late. So I thought, so did many around me. I was just in that bad of a condition. But the capability of human beings and the nature of life taught me a simple truth: I was wrong. I was stronger than I thought I was; we are stronger than we think we are. Give yourself another chance.

I was shot multiple times. Many years later, as I am writing this book, I am alive and well. The next time you think you can't remember the story of me (Raz Coco). If I survived, I have no doubt that you can too.

But it wasn't over for Raz Coco, just the mere beginning.

6

Vengeance

"When a good guy loses his patience, the devil shivers."

From all the thoughts I had during my time of despair, one thought in particular was of an inevitable nature. Do you let go or follow through? Time after time again, this is the question I asked myself. I was always in the midst of two major decisions. Which one was I to manifest? Listen, "Revenge is a double-edged sword." These philosophies are for those who read stories and watch movies or those who are not in a position to do anything about it—that, or, of course, those who learn it the hard way. After I started to recover, I wasn't perfect nor anywhere close to who I used to be, but I was better. Much better than when I first came to the hospital. With recovery, with power, came my sense of ego. Then, of course, there were my friends, who were already going back and forth with the other gang and had the intent to avenge me. They were on about this for a while. While at first, when I didn't know if I'd ever be able to walk again, I never felt the need to do something and wanted to let go. But now, it was different. I felt a deep sense of anger about what they had done to me. That I did not deserve any of this, and that Usman would have to pay for what he did. I couldn't walk properly and was in no position to fight, yet my friends were adamant to take action. That I would not have to do anything, and they would take care of everything else. In hindsight, it was this opportunity that shined a vengeful light onto me, that there was a way I could get back to the person who put me in this position.

Osman had turned himself in the same day he had pointed his gun at me but got out soon enough. Each and every single day, the need to do something and standing up for myself was getting to me.

My anger slowly started to build up the need to take action. However, it was not just the past that I kept coming back to. The city where I lived was pretty small at the time, and it was quite common to run into people you knew of. I had seen Usman around here and there and felt my anger boiling up each time I did. He had, along with his gang, built quite the reputation based on what they did to me; people were scared of them, and they were considered a serious gang. Once, I remember running into Usman and his gang outside of a club while I was still on crutches. He and his goons had the audacity to laugh at me while making idiotic gestures. Another time, they literally tried to run me over by their car while I was on my way to physio. They would also come to our school and point guns at students; the same happened at my graduation. The question I was kept on being asked was: What was I going to do about it? Again and again, this question was repeated to me while I formulated answers. It's one of those things where one finds themselves in a tricky situation. You can't just say that you'll do nothing; others will think less of you and run you over. They'll consider you a pushover because, at the end of the day, none of those people went through what I did. For a while, I was in a place of thankfulness; I was happy to be alive, and I told everyone that it was better to let go. But the constant poking by Usman and his goons, along with my friends and the encouragement of others to take action, all boiled to the surface. Enough was enough. We needed to act.

It was one of these days that I received a phone call at 5 am in the morning. Another unfortunate incident had occurred as my friend on the other line told me how a friend from our group was stabbed in the heart by some white guys. They had gone to this club and found trouble; a fight had broken out. Now, these guys had started to keep knives with them; needless to say, they did not want a fate similar to mine. So when the fight broke out, guys got stabbed, and my homie Issac was killed. This devastation did nothing but further boil my rage to the surface.

While we were all devastated and angry, Both Sam and Jomo felt guilty about the loss of our friend. They were all involved in hurting one of the white guys. They had started to run when the other group came at them, and for the most part, Sam was the target. He was nearly almost caught when Issac turned around to save him and was stabbed to death. Issac's girl was pregnant, and he had to leave this world, leaving behind a daughter who would soon grow up without a father to look after her. Both these guys were not in a good place and carried a sense of guilt that never seemed to let go of you till the end of your days. A demon in the back of your mind that never stops haunting you, as you can never help but think that you've somehow skipped death by an unfortunate offering of another. It is even more haunting when it is a loved one. It seemed as if all the harmony our little town once knew had been invaded and infected by utter evil. Chaos was everywhere, and people all around worried for the sake of themself and their family's safety. We had become a gang-bred town dominated by a variety of Asian gangs, white gangs, black gangs, Indian gangs, and Lebanese gangs. The end goal? The most common goal of all is money. There were great opportunities in the oil fields, and it was at the centre of interest for these gangs. Usman was the top-of-the-chain gangster everyone feared and respected now more than ever, as no one wanted to suffer as I did. For me, being the reason he was able to establish such dominance was the cherry on top of all my despair. We were all equally shook, as a combination of emotions all not so healthy filled our minds. Too much had happened, and really, nothing else was important anymore. It was time to take revenge.

Motive: Vengeance.
Targets: Usman, The White Knights (White gang.)
Intent: Murder.

A group of friends had now decided to join hands and form a gang of ourselves. More so a hit squad than a gang. The idea was to plan, strategize, and tactically strike with little to no possible repercussions. We started to think. What can we do? To keep myself out of visible trouble, I started working with my father, driving a small truck and helping the family with thoughts so dark that words would not do justice. Sam and Jomo did not have any jobs at this time. We would meet at our shop and consider any and all ways to do what we deemed necessary. We had established that, before anything else, guns were an absolute necessity. We also adapted to the first rule of fight club: no one was to know what we had going on. NO ONE. More than anything else, we made a pact that no one would ever hurt us ever again. I felt the need to take charge as I definitely was the most motivated based on what had been done to me. I had some resources behind me as well, so I decided to take charge.

During this time, we were at a club where the white knights just so happened to be. Someone pointed at one of their guys as one who helped kill Isaac. At the time, none of us were actually aware as to who killed Isaac. We knew that there were three guys who did the stabbing, but nobody really knew who actually killed him. Anywho, one of the three names was at this club that night, and so we were called to that club. It wasn't just us; there were 20 of us. Not long before, we got a hold of him outside and wrecked him up pretty bad. Some of the guys also went a step ahead to rob him. This guy was a drug dealer and was loaded. So they got some money out of him while he was left in a pool of his own blood. We all reap what we sow. Sow the wind, reap the whirlwind. Yet such matters of life were foreign to kids of our age, especially youngsters involved in gang life. For us, this was just the beginning, an initiation that went well.

Meanwhile, we were not the only people who opposed Usman. They were predominantly a Muslim group and went back and forth with some Sikh guys and an Indian gang. Usman's brother, Adam, was more involved in fighting against these groups. Adam, Usman's younger brother, seemed to be really interested and motivated to follow in his brother's footsteps.

Not long before, Jomo had an idea. The first task was to get guns. He knew a group that he used to hang out with and one guy in particular, Tin, caught his eye. They had what we needed. So, we decided to take action. We located this guy and followed him to the destination suspected to be loaded with weaponry. We broke in, entered this guy's residence, and found what we were looking for—lots and lots of guns. We filled a whole hockey bag with shotguns, rifles, handguns, and bullets.

After gaining possession of a whole range of weaponry, we were happy. Excited for what we had managed to get a hold of, and eager to make use of it. We cut off the long-barrelled shotgun and kept the handguns with us to protect ourselves. However, there was no inclination to just go ahead and conduct a shootout at a local club; the last thing we wanted was to get caught. So we came up with a plan. After some key observation and assessment, we came to the conclusion that it had to happen on their way to the club or back, as they spent so much time there hanging out. Even though everyone knew where Usman lived, we did not find it wise to shoot him dead on his porch, which would inevitably lead to one of his goons doing the same to us, getting our families unnecessarily involved. The situation was trickier than it may sound, primarily because even though we did not want anyone to know it was us, we also wanted to establish a certain dominance for others to comprehend our capability and put some respect for our names. We also established that he had to be caught off guard. Usman was flashy, in your-face, I don't care kind of a guy, an individual so out and about that everyone could tell you where they're at. By this time, almost everyone had a cellphone, and so we would get these calls from guys we were friendly with, as to where Usman was at a given time. Myself, Sam and Jomo were the shooters, while other kids who were with us would help us out by keeping us informed. The clueless girls would let us take their cars as we would switch the license plates of their cars and would go out at night time, looking for these guys with our hockey bag filled with weaponry.

I'd never shot a gun before we got a hold of them. After being at the unfortunate end of one, I was almost scared of it and so needed to practice and befriend it, though easier said than done. I remember watching Will Smith's *Bad Boys,* in which one of the guys got shot in the leg yet got the girl and managed to save the day, which the younger me sort of empathized with. When watching movies, we often forget the difference between watching a movie and getting shot in real life. Life requires you to take charge and ownership of your life. Sitting in the passenger seat while another takes charge of the steering wheel was never worth it. It didn't take long for me to build the confidence to not only start carrying a gun but also practice and get our aims strong. I grew quite comfortable using a gun. I wouldn't say we were great shooters, but enough to get the job done. We were yet to build comfort with the shotgun, since it heavily kicked back after it shot.

Sam was the timid one of the group, Jomo was the more aggressive one and probably the most experienced and then there was me. Ultimately, I saw this as my revenge path and wanted to be a part of everything and do whatever I could. I didn't want to be just the shooter, but I wanted to help in any way possible. I had stopped going to school, something I never thought I'd be doing, yet life had other plans. We basked in the glory and power the guns brought us as we roamed around the city, feeling like superheroes. I had gotten a holster; the idea was simple. Anyone who stepped into me would instantly meet his maker. I was ready.

During these times of chaos, I was dating this girl. Once, we were hanging out when I noticed these guys obnoxiously staring at my girl. Any other day, I would take my girl and walk away. But with this gun in my waste, I wanted to take them out. This burning desire could manifest in a matter of seconds. I was just looking for an excuse to pull out my gun and do what I had been preparing for. Though it would be foolish of me to say that a sense of morality is what stopped me, more than the fact that I knew I needed to be careful. My enemy was one guy, and so I swallowed this burning sensation that tingled my ego. I also knew I needed to be careful due to an incident a while back at a club. Once again me, Jomo, Sam and some girls we used to hang out with; these ladies were cool and quite intelligent and also used to help us out. We were in Lisa's car and rolled up to quite the scene, a crazy rave party where the common theme was either molly or ecstasy, if not both, and danced all night long. Amongst all this, we spotted Usman, yet he wasn't alone. Amongst his other goons, I saw my shooter, the guy they called Camel. Once we entered this club, Usman started his usual taunts from a distance, showing me the middle finger, telling us to leave and that something was going to happen to me to try to intimidate me. But it was different this time, we were not scared, and were ready to go if need be, our shotguns were ready in the back seat of the car we came in. After his taunts, we decided to take action.

Later that night, while Usman was still inside, we came outside, and an opportunity presented itself as we noticed Usman's car through his number plate, which we instantly recognized. Though what appealed to us and me in specific, was the person inside that car. It was Camel, the kid who pulled the trigger on me over and over. We grabbed our black ski masks and shotguns, while Camel was passed out in Usman's car probably due to drugs. We made our way to his car in an attempt to shoot Camel when Usman came outside and saw us. Even though we had masks on, he knew who we were. He threw us a sign indicating that we should shoot Camel. This is the sort of man he was.

Jomo looks at me and tells me to shoot him. This was my chance. The soul of the man who attacked me with no mercy and not too long ago was mine for the taking, just a pull of a trigger away. But now that Usman wanted us to shoot him, I could not do it. I did not want the slave who was following his master's orders, and I wanted the kingpin. The girls we came with had also come out by this time and were looking at us. We decided to retreat. We got back into the car and took off, dropped the girls off and went back to our homes.

This was not the only incident, and there were many times we would plan to kill Usman but could not due to one reason or the other. Once we were told that Usman would be going through this road late at night, we had the car and were ready to make the move. The idea was simple: make use of the dark night and shoot him passing by. That didn't work out, and went against our favor. I was driving, and the plan was for Sam to shoot him. Yet, for whatever reason, he could not do it. Not only that, Usman saw our faces when we passed by, as that was the day I believe that Usman understood that we were after him.

Not long after this, these guys rolled up on me. I was alone this time around while Usman was with Camel and another one of his guys. They were passing by while making these hand gestures at me, like pointing his hand like a gun, trying to tell me that he'd shot me and whatnot. I had my gun with me and was not afraid to take action. I remember quite vividly how fast they bolted when I took my gun out and pointed it at them. It was clear that they did not expect that. Also, it was made clear to them that we carried, and that they could no longer try to bully us around when they seemed fitting. I wouldn't lie, it felt good.

Looking back, while there is no doubt that the path I chose to pursue was the wrong one, I also fail to see how a kid in that situation and environment would do anything else. None of us had even reached the age of 21, and the occurrences of our surroundings weighed so heavily that we were molded to become who we were. After almost losing my life and being stuck to the confines of the beds of a hospital and my own household, with Usman still trying to push us around, it almost felt like I manifested my inevitable destiny. Maybe I could have chosen another path, given there was no guarantee that my friends and I would have made it out alive. Sometimes, the only way to move on is to go further ahead. Or at least, it would seem to someone in that situation, especially when you are that young and so much has happened to you. While yes, there was no assurance that if I took on a path of forgiveness, life would have been better, the fact that I did not find out what was at the end of that path; the path less taken by the path of morality, would have made all the difference.

7

A Near Miss

Murder. We have all thought about it at some point in our lives. Hypothetical for most, stemming from anger or frustration against an individual. This feeling has a vast array of translations, from growing insecure to knocking one out, plotting against them, tucking the feeling inside and letting it boil, move on, or simply go for the kill. But what makes you cross that unlawful line? While the core of this decision does indeed consist of innate habits of rage and temperament, it also consists of your circumstances. Something that drives you to the brink of such an abyss that you find yourself having such thoughts. I was at the brink of such an abyss when I did not know if I would ever be the man I once was if I'd ever be able to live again. Now, I was ready to make the move, and I was ready to take revenge. But alas, thought and manifestations are two different planes. Planning to kill someone is different than killing someone. We had opportunities, but it never happened. I was growing frustrated.

Our motive was vivid to the enemy. In a way, we felt mocked for not being able to do the job. We could see in hindsight why him getting away that night was better for us. Yet, with each passing day, the need to extract our revenge grew within us. We were growing hungry, and the fact that he could hurt us just as much and that perhaps he was plotting to do so did not matter. Safety was not our main priority at this point in time; it was blood. All in all, war had been declared.

Often our subconscious falls prey to our conscious decisions. I was having these dreams where I was imprisoned. Consciously and partially due to my subconscious dreams, I knew my decision would lead me to an unfortunate end. But it did not matter. I was content with letting my decision to hurt another, change my life. Me and my group were aware of this situation and had a mutual understanding that every meeting we had could be the last one. It's a weird way of saying goodbye.

At this point, my friends had found employment, and we were all working, something that I quite enjoyed. I was working for my father's company, driving a truck. We would all meet after our shifts at night to discuss our plans for the future.

During this time, there was a lot of back and forth. There were a few incidents where we would get calls from our friends at school, who would either be at the wrong end of the stick with Usman and his goons, or they simply spotted the gang. They knew who to call. Whenever the call came, we rushed down to the school, ready to rage war. But Usman and his gang stayed low for the most part and would almost always get away and escape an altercation with us.

Boxing Day is a Canadian holiday celebrated the day after Christmas, occurring on the second day of Christmastide. Originating as a holiday to give gifts to the poor, Boxing Day is now primarily known as a shopping holiday. My friends and I were to go to one of these sales in Edmonton, and Usman and his group were there as well. Crews would often hang tight and almost never separate from one another, so did we and Usman's gang. You being spotted alone could make all the difference in life and death situations. We didn't see their crew for ourselves; we received a call from one of our friends. My friends immediately asked if we should act and do something about it. My mind immediately flashed back to a recent incident where someone was stabbed in the head.

We prepared ourselves. I recall packing our hockey bag of guns to take with us in the vehicle. We were ready to attack. Unfortunately, they were gone by the time we reached. Their luck because, at this point, we could care less about any repercussions. God works in mysterious ways. Perhaps these little incidents were an indication that we were not the ones responsible for manifesting Usman and his gang's karma. For what we sow, we reap. But such philosophies have too much weight for young blood out on vengeance. For us, each passing day was a day near to Usman's rightful demise.

We crossed each other's paths quite often. Multiple drive-bys, we would chase them, but they would get away. This went on for a while. Once, I took a friend with me to a local club for a celebration. The clueless girls were with me. Not long before, I spotted Usman and his goons. Not only did I see them, but they saw me, too; eye contact was made. My team was not with me at this point in time. I could not help but consider getting away and avoiding the situation altogether. There was no need for me to be surrounded by a pack of wolves ready to attack. But a young man's ego is bold and wild—a lot of decisions and not a lot of time to think. I had my gun on me and thought to take care of the situation myself. At this point, people had figured that the south side's two enemies were at the same place. Some of their wannabes came up to me and tried to intimidate me to leave, thinking that it would be better, given I was outnumbered. I found a phone and called my friends using the code. "Sisters" was the codename for our hockey bag of weaponry. I was ready and didn't mind having my back against the wall. I did hope that my friends made it on time. I also did not feel the need to make the first move, so I waited patiently.

Not long before Usman, Camel, and Miles, the guy who drove Camel to shoot me, came toward me and a gang of around eight members. They started calling out names in an attempt to bully me. Trying to intimidate me, calling me bitch and saying that I should leave, that I knew what they were capable of. He was no longer low-key and was quite loud in an attempt to assert dominance and capture attention. The lady friend of mine I was with had no idea what was going on. Needless to say, she had no idea about the loaded gun I had earlier slipped inside her bag. I took the gun out of the bag and kept it with me. I was patient; I was ready to shoot him, but only if he attacked me first. When I didn't budge to his insults, he pulled out his gun and pointed it at me. I knew the time had come. But if I reached for my gun, he would shoot me. I was now in a tricky situation. I needed to figure something out quickly.

I decided to play possum. Backing up with my hands by my side and the words "Please don't hurt me," I acted out a surrender. Continuing to play possum, I turned around, giving him my back as I acted in fear, continuing the act in an attempt to quickly grab my gun without being vividly noticed. I knew that I might possibly die and never get this opportunity again or an opportunity at anything ever again. But death did not scare me. I knew it was now or never. I went for it. I took out the gun, held it behind my back, and turned to Usman, a completely different person. I stood up tall and looked deep into his eyes.

"What the fuck did you say, you bitch?"

Years of rage glared in my eyes. He stepped back. I knew he could see it in my eyes. I was not a man afraid. I sensed his fear. A few steps back was not enough. Too much was taken from me. I was the one who was taunting him now. I'd be lying if I said it didn't feel good. So I talk shit to him in front of his whole crew and the crowd. He tried to get to his weapon, so I grabbed his jacket while mocking him. That big mouth of his had to be shut. I put my gun right to his mouth and pinned him down. It was time. The man I was obsessed with killing was in front of the wrong end of the gun, and everybody was watching. How dare this man do to me what he did. How dare he take valuable years out of my life, not knowing if I'd ever be normal again. Those endless nights in the hospital, I suffered in pain and agony. The feeling of never being able to walk again. Never being able to fuck. Not getting to live life fully again. Laying down in a dark room of the hospital, thinking what would happen to me. Scared out of my fucking mind. All that my family went through in those stressful times. All because of nothing. I did not deserve anything this man did to me. Yet he did it, nevertheless. He did not know, nor did he care about the repercussions of what it would be like for my family on my unfortunate demise. He did not care about what it would be like for me if I barely made it alive. He did not care about anything but himself, his ego, and his self-respect. He was the cause of all my bottled-up rage, hate, and pain. So yeah, I pulled the fucking trigger.

I was in a trance. I saw his eyes roll back as he fell down backward on the floor. After a brief moment of silence, the crowd realized what just happened and started to scream in havoc. Everybody was scared of me, and I was now a menace. For the first time, I wasn't a victim, and power never tasted so good. I noticed Camel realizing the situation and trying to make a run for it. At this point, I had no doubt in my mind that I could take him out as well. Everybody scattered to escape me, but I went after Camel, who ducked under a nearby table. Again, this was his lucky day, and this time, he wasn't drugged up and sleeping in a car; this time, I had him on the run, just like when he gunned me down, running away from him.

Ready to take my revenge, I pointed the gun at him and pulled the trigger, but nothing came out. At this point, everyone was rushing out of the club's entrance. I tried to make a run for it, shoving people out of my way, the same people who were running away from the kid with the gun in his hand. I was almost at the door when a tall, muscled white guy with a ponytail came from behind me, spun me around, and pinned me to the wall beside the door. I was surprised that my enemies would attack me from behind, knowing I had a gun. I immediately pointed my weapon toward him, but the gun was still not working. In the midst of him realizing I was about to kill him while I was considering that this guy was not an enemy but just the club bouncer and the fact that my gun was still not working, I asked this guy to let me go. I told him that he could have the gun and that I just needed to get out of there. In the midst of this chaos, he shouted back at me that he could not let me go while I was trying to convince him to let me be and that it was not safe. Suddenly, the window behind me crashed, and I feared the enemy had me in their targets. Behind the hero bouncer, I saw someone throwing pool balls at us, aiming for our heads. I noticed them to be Usman's crew, throwing the balls as hard as they could, breaking the windows behind me. I handed the gun to the bouncer as I watched him fear for his life, this time letting me go. I bolted outside the bar.

As soon as I stepped outside, I heard, "Freeze! Put your hands up!" I did and told them immediately that I did not have the gun. Not knowing what they understood, they told me to go. I felt relieved and made a run for it when the bouncer stepped outside the bar's entrance with the gun in his hand. The police officer points his gun at him, asking him to do the same. The bouncer shouted, "I am just the bouncer; it's him!" pointing in my direction. The officer points his gun back at me and orders me to get to the ground. I surrendered. The officer put me in his car. I noticed people around the bar chanting my name while I was hinting at them to stop saying my name. "LESLIE, LESLIE, LESLIE, LESLIE….." I was in a deep trance and did not have any particular thoughts at this point in time. I knew what I did but did not have the time to make something out of it. I just knew that I shot Usman. I shot him in the face, and so I knew he was dead. I just killed a man and did not feel much of anything, not at that point in time. The adrenaline was perhaps to blame, or a sense of justice, attaining vengeance, or something else. How does it feel to take someone's life? I wish I could tell you. The next thing I noticed outside the cop car's window was Usman, barely alive, walking out and leaning on the shoulders of his goons.

In utter confusion, a sense of fear sent chills through my body, I couldn't believe what I was seeing. I had to consider the fact that perhaps I had killed someone else. On close attention, I realized that it was Usman. I kept looking in a complete state of shock. How is this possible? I kept asking myself while utterly confused. I did not know what to make of it. Is it possible to survive after a shot in the face? This was mind-boggling to young me, and there was nothing I could do with my hands cuffed sitting in the back seat of the cop's car.

At this point, I wasn't glad that he survived and that I'd be safe from any consequences that come along with murder. I couldn't care less about the consequences; I wanted this man dead. Now I was being driven to the police station while that man was in an ambulance. I felt a bunch of emotions, all overpowering each other, with Usman's survival being the cherry on top. A sense of pride for standing up for myself and it ending with my name being chanted across the crime scene. A state of shock and rage for him surviving, with some fear for the consequences lurking in the background. I felt quite a lot, yet nothing at all. I call it the calm after the storm.

Victim's family appalled at barroom killer's jail sentence

"(Freeman) could have picked up a pool cue but no, he had to pick up that knife and stab somebody."

Moreau called the fact that Freeman used a knife an aggravating factor in the case and said a stiff sentence is needed to deter armed bar fights.

"A stern message has to be sent to those who enter barroom brawls and introduce weapons," said Moreau, who also tagged Freeman with a 10-year firearms prohibition.

Freeman, who had argued the stabbing at Fabio's Place, 10625 51 Ave., was done in self-defence, said Tuesday that he did not accept the manslaughter conviction.

Man to stand trial for mall shooting

The victim of a 1996 shooting at a south Edmonton mall was committed to stand trial yesterday on a charge of attempted murder for allegedly shooting another man.

Provincial court Judge Russell Dzenick ordered Leslie Cletus Raymond, 21, to appear at the Dec. 8 Court of Queen's Bench arraignments to set a trial date following a two-day preliminary hearing.

Court heard earlier Raymond allegedly shot at Usman Pervez, 21, with a Colt .45-calibre semi-automatic handgun at the Windmill Bar and Grill at Millbourne Shopping Centre on March 27.

The alleged shooting was done in front of about 200 witnesses and Raymond was nabbed by bar staff shortly after.

Pervez survived the shooting but ended up with a bullet

Court heard that police allege Pervez is the head of a gang called the Browns, who are squabbling with a group called the Blacks. Raymond is an alleged member of the Blacks.

Raymond denies belonging to a gang.

Pervez, who was sentenced to eight months in jail on Oct. 20 after pleading guilty to selling a pound of pot to an undercover police officer, said he has become a new man since being shot in the mouth.

Defence lawyer Walter Raponi said when Pervez "ate a bullet" it gave him a "life-changing experience" which has set him on a crime-free path. Raponi also said Pervez is missing part of his jaw and several teeth and needs to have a bone transplant from his hip to repair the damage.

Raymond is also charged with pointing a firearm, possession of a restricted weapon, possession of a restricted weapon with the serial number removed and possession of an unregistered firearm.

Despite being hit five times, Raymond survived a brazen daytime shooting at Southgate Shopping Centre on July 4, 1996.

8

Criminal

It was moments after my hands had been cuffed behind my back, a police officer pushing my head down, forcing me harshly towards the backseat door of the police car. Like I said, I had an adrenaline rush that was quite unlike anything I had experienced before. The situation offered me a position of power and revenge. Yet, for someone who had nearly or just committed first-degree murder, I was oddly calm. At that moment, however, I was not sure if this calm after the storm was because I was genuinely at ease with what I had done or if it was a sense of shock which prevented my consciousness from registering what I had just subconsciously done, what it had resulted in and how that would impact the rest of my life. As I was being taken to the police station, it resonated in my head merely as if I were locating from one place to another in a cab while being drunk. You know how one might be almost passed out on their way home from a party in what we resonate within the current day as an Uber. I genuinely felt like I was being chaperoned home. Except I had committed a borderline heinous crime in the eyes of the law, and I was going anywhere but home. Perhaps the one place that was meant to feel least like home. It's different, you know when you go to jail for the first time in your life.

Oddly enough, aside from the rational acknowledgment in my head that I was going to atone for my crime and, depending on whether or not my mortal enemy had made it out alive, perhaps an eternity in jail, I felt nothing. No remorse, sadness, a harbinger of doom, depression, nothing. I could resonate with the feeling of being unrightfully scolded by the teacher for standing up to them for a legitimate mistake and issue on their part and was hence being sent to the principal's office because I had not done anything wrong. I had nothing to fear. For me, I served my part in Usman's karma, I avenged his wrongdoing and brought myself a sense of justice. But then again, I had seen him walking out alive, and so I did not know what to make out of my decision other than the fact that it felt great. After a few futile attempts of trying to fish for emotions of regret and sadness, I gave up. It was official, and I did not feel anything except a sense of having done what was right.

The ride was not that long, considering I had solely been going back and forth in my head and my own thoughts. The initial shock from the incident started to wear away slowly and not kindly. I was worried about my family. A little thought in my head told me they did not deserve to have gone through what they did and what they possibly will. It pained me to think of the sorrow I would once again put them through, but I kept assuring myself I did what had to be done and that they would surely understand. If anything, my parents and family were the main people who suffered directly from the attack I suffered and the aftermath of the event for the years after. True, while I was agonizing in pain and in the mental effects of not being able to do many things the way I would have, I tried imagining life from their perspective, my family, acknowledging being related to a gangster who had committed possible murder and was on trial for it, alongside being associated with other public shootings. Some part of me, in that short time period being in the police car, simply thought that I had brought shame on my family and wondered what they had even done in the first place to deserve me and my decisions. Despite all these thoughts, I finally settled on acknowledging that all this was forced. What I was really feeling at that moment was a surreal sense of calm. As confused as I was, I let that feeling of calmness wash over me as I finally stepped into the police station. Scared, needless to say, but calm.

When I finally got there, a police officer wanted to contact my parents to bring me a fresh set of clothes because they wanted to confiscate my outfit as evidence. I assumed it was for gunpowder residue, among other obvious facets like DNA and blood. I did not have the gun I shot Usman with because when I tried to leave the club, pleading to the bouncer to let me go, he held onto me at the entrance and took my gun, which he eventually and responsibly gave to the police later. Of course, there was no denying that I was the shooter. I suppose they still needed my clothes as evidence as part of the protocol. Even though I had ever so slightly been worrying about my parent's reaction to this newfound crisis I brought upon us, I called them. My mother picked up the phone, and I merely told her that I had been arrested for a shooting. The next part is why I think I have truly been blessed with amazing parents. My mother came over immediately with a fresh set of clothes. Since they had not booked me yet, I was not to be put in a prison uniform. Even after I was to be booked, I'd be placed on a 23-hour lockdown before any legal proceeds were made.

My mother was not mad at all. Or so it seemed. Neither were the rest of my family. They did not panic, were tense nor grieving in any way. In fact, they understood. They knew why I did what I did. They saw my pain and suffering for years, and they were with me throughout all of it. In addition to that, they may not have supported my decision, but they stood with me and helped me through my predicament in emotionally uplifting ways. They knew my strength was unquestionable, given what I had already been through from a young age.

My mother is a strong woman, and I like to think I got my courage and strength from her. Even when I was shot, I could not imagine the pain she must have gone through for me, and there were moments that followed after the shooting when I did not know if I would live again. I'm sure she did, too. The nature of that thought is of inevitability. But she never showed any distressed agony and did her best to keep my spirits high. She assured me time and time again that we were going to get through this together. And she was true to her word.

Back at the police station where I was held, the environment around me was confusing, to say the least. Despite the fact that prison is full of people who've committed an array of crimes when a possible newbie felon comes in, he might get somewhat bullied in exchange for the prisoners' boredom and a lack of a better hobby. In my case, however, I sensed that everyone, including the officers themselves, acknowledged me with an air of respect. It was almost as if they not only respected the intent behind my crime, given that quite a few of them knew my history with Usman, but they also admired my courage in standing up to him. It was odd. I did not know that the other inmates respected me just as much until later.

So, the police booked me at the precinct and then had to take me down to a place that they called the Remand Center, which was basically a local jail or the county jail. The Remand was overcrowded, and there were no proper holding cells at the time. The police force wasn't clear on what to do with me, so I was sent to the high-profile unit. Eventually, I was charged with two attempted murders and a whole leaf of gun possessions, amongst other smaller charges.

I remember that night. There was no jail nor judge that I could see until the next morning. My lawyer also advised me not to see one because, despite it being my first time being charged for anything, the charges were extreme. I had seen Usman alive momentarily, but there was no actual surety that he had made it out alive. So it was unclear if my charges were for murder, and we all generically knew what the sentences for those look like.

At the end of the day, attempted murder still shares the same destination as a proper one, so they ended up sending me to jail anyway. I was sent there directly. I recall one of the officers asking if I wanted to buy cigarettes. I was going to be here for a while anyway, and it was that pack that started my smoking habit for the many years to come. By then, I also realized that they liked and respected me. Soon, they gave me my prison attire. It was a blue jumpsuit and a toothbrush, and then I was taken to my designated cell. This cell was particularly for those with extreme charges. All the hardcore criminals housed together, and then me. I was a first-time offender. What I had been charged with was not a minor crime, and the cherry on top was that it all happened in public. The story about the ongoing feud with Usman had been a story that the public had been following for a while. It was all on the news the following morning, and somehow, there were other big names involved. Even back in 99 'when Usman had hired a hitman to take me down, the news had taken various versions when it had been broadcast to the public media. Now, once again, the same names were in the papers, except the hunted was now the hunter, which intrigued the masses.

Not long before, it all started to register. It was about 23 hours in when an inkling of fear tickled down my spine, and I knew why. I was locked up with some of the most hardcore criminals in the area. Even though I was somewhat of a gangster myself, most of them were serial criminals and were wanted for crimes beyond my imagination. I remember when I was entering the vicinity, and I saw two guys screaming and yelling death threats at each other. A part of me knew their threats were not in vain. There were different types of people in jail, huge, hunky native men, short but fierce-looking Asian men, black and brown men who were abnormally large and intimidating, and a big husky Aboriginal guy. As I was passing by, one of them yelled.

"Hey, that's Les Ray!"

A part of me sank deeply into the depths of my chest, right into my stomach. The last thing I wanted was to be harassed by a bunch of people who had no empathy or emotion whatsoever. But a feeling inside me told me I'd be fine. I turned to that guy who had called out my name, and we exchanged a few words that got my attention. He told me that there was about 20 grand on my head. I was sure that the news had spread like wildfire and that more people knew about the incident than I'd wanted. Whatever the news was, it had spread incredibly fast despite the fact that back in the day, there was no social media and whatnot. It had not even been 24 hours yet. DAMN. Time seemed limited. There were some other gangsters nearby, one I recognized from the newspaper. The others would introduce themselves. The same Asian gang member had put a man in the emergency room solely because he had been talking to his girlfriend. I recall a particular time I considered him an asshole. So, I saw him coming towards me, his expression almost unreadable yet intimidating. I thought I should be scared, but more so, intrigued by what route he would take in conversing with me.

He came over and introduced himself as Vincent Gambella. He told me he was the leader of his Asian Gang, which I knew a bit about. I knew this man was no joke. He told me he admired what I had done and that I had his respect. I was stunned for a moment or two. But then again, this seemed to be the general buzz around me, and for some reason, I was a hero for most, which made sense. Gambella offered to let me know the rules and told me how things worked here. In that particular moment, perhaps because of the shock of the events within the past few hours, my gut and instinct were empty, as if they had nothing to offer me. This man beat another man, turning him into a vegetable for reasons that didn't make sense to me, so of course, I was weighing the options of what such a situation could mean. Either he genuinely took a liking to me, or he was trying to take advantage of my naiveté and newness. Either way, I did not have much choice, so I accepted his seemingly warm gesture.

A lot of inmates seemed to think that I was brave for not chickening out and skipping town as many cowards would do when the police got involved. They secretly applauded the fact that I stood my ground. Though I did not need their validation to elevate my self-esteem, I already knew what I did was nothing but be true to myself and my dignity. They assured me that we are all criminals, but these inmates are the ones who get caught. They knew that my crime of passion was worth it, and they stood by that. I guess that was one thing I did need to tell myself. Like I said, I wasn't particularly looking for validation, but it was better to be respected than to be on the wrong side of the tracks with these guys. I wasn't as strong or experienced in the dark ways of prison as the rest of these guys were. But that validation did, however, validate me in some sense. For any and all feelings of guilt did fade away quite a bit, the perspective of being courageous and avenging myself was a point of view that took power in me, pushing down any feelings of agony for the destination I had ended up at. See, many chose the option to walk away, not battle an outside force that has wronged them. They end up with a building sense of anger and frustration that eats away at their soul bit by bit till the day they die. It speeds up your ageing process, and these feelings of frustration harm the ones around you. For me, yeah, I was in jail. But I was also fulfilled. Looking back, if I had another chance, I probably would end up making the same choice again. There are pros and cons to every decision. Choose your poison wisely. Choose the poison you can live with.

Because I did just that, and now live alive and well enough to tell the tale with a bright future to look for and no demons to hold me back. I left my demons behind me when I pulled the trigger.

9

An Artist, Emerged

Even though I was held at the maximum-security unit, I was a source of comfort for a lot of the inmates and prison guards. The security personnel were not allowed any cigarettes, but we were. I had the money and resources and put it towards my canteen. So, I built a good relationship with many just listening to the stories and advice of men older than me. Inmates are usually assigned chores, and every time I was given a cleaning chore, it meant I got to stay out longer than the assigned hours as per the regulations. All of this had happened only within a span of 24 hours.

Since the cigarette provision I had dealt with became increasingly popular, I was surrounded by quite a lot of interesting individuals. I got to hear tales about their notorious criminal lives, and so much was beyond my imagination. I met a man named Felix. He was a biker and belonged to a bike gang called the *Hell's Angels*. Although, I don't even know if that was true. Regardless, it is what he claimed to be, linking himself to illegal activities planned by the likes of gangsters on motorcycles. He would tell me stories and specific details, as well as different events related to his gang culture. Not only did he submerge me in his own personal life, choices, relationships, and eventful happenstance, but he also told me quite a lot about generalized biker gang life and how it differs from other gangs. These sessions of talking and listening to veteran gang members of different cultures and backgrounds became almost educational for me. It was like a counselling session for the streets. It was somewhat relieving and appreciated. Plus, the guys loved telling me their stories because I was young, and they wanted to help out. A youngster who listens when a wise man talks. They did not wish for people who would one-up them when need be but rather a neutral junior who would enjoy the tales. And, like I said, I would give them cigarettes, which would make them all happy. And they all kind of respected me, so we got along.

I vividly remember the night I had been booked and slept like a baby. It was quite odd. It was also something the other inmates had not seen in a while, especially for someone who was in jail for the very first time and at a young age. In my head, my reasoning was that I was simply exhausted after the day's events. Yes, at one point in time, my adrenaline had reached a peak that I had never quite felt or seen before. But that night, I felt overly drained and exhausted. The happenstance began to wash over me like a quilted duvet as I slipped into a velvet-soft, deep state of sleep. The next morning was different.

I had no idea whatsoever where I was. Everything felt like a terribly long and detailed nightmare. If I just took a turn and went back to sleep, I might dream of something better. Or better yet, somehow, wake up. There was no attempted murder, no jail, just the comfortable bed in my parent's house. The second startle was perhaps quite the physically painful jerk. But then, it kicked in, finally, so I was not in my house and neither in my bed. I was in prison!

That too In a high-security cell, and I had most of the time of my 23-hour hold ahead of me. The time I had spent in there was merely the tip of the iceberg. Every inmate had only about 1 hour of roaming time. Only the cleaners got an extra two or three, which is why I actively participated in cleaning duties. I would mop and broom, followed by sneaking cigarettes into the cellmate's shells. It was quite the process. This also largely depended on whether the guards liked you, and I need not repeat, I was already well-liked by prisoners, criminals, and guards alike because I did my job and kept the unit happy.

There is a rule in this criminal life. Regardless of whether a particular gangster likes you or not, if the leader of the gang is fond of you and thinks that you are alright, the rest of the gang cannot harm you. I knew this, and hence, it was the ethic I adopted. I did not pick fights on my own. I was not much trouble to anyone, and it was hard to say if anyone aside from Usman and his men disliked me at all. However, the idea was to try to get close to the gang leaders, which I did.

It might shock many to know that I was in jail for two years before my court hearing. I applied for bail the first time, but it was denied. I pleaded for bail a second time, and yet again, I was dismissed. Despite the fact that several people understood my case, the judge informed us that he denied us bail because my case was too public. Most of the public had their eyes on my sentence and my fate. Not only had this incident been well known around town, but the incident where I had been shot too and has been outrageously publicized by the media. Most of the people who had heard of the story now knew that the shooter, in this case, was the same Les Ray. If I were granted bail, I would still be under some house arrest. However, the judge feared that would anger men on both sides, in addition to my release, would result in a public massacre and execution on the streets. Apart from that, the state wanted to ensure my safety, so keeping me in there was the only way they could ensure my well-being, and of course, the well-being of others of my opposition, against me.

Before my first appearance in court, I had already been in jail for approximately six months. I had a total of two years of putting together my case, piece by piece. An appeal for bail would be denied, and then until the next holding, I would go back to jail and stay there. Since there was a holding every week, the process of getting rejected and re-appealing again took mostly about a week. Throughout this time, my co-gang members, my friends from school, and many other individuals showed me their support by writing letters to me. They wrote long essay-like paragraphs about how they admired my strength and how well my family seemed to be holding up despite these hard times, how we set a great example for individuals and families who were going through hard times like us due to the short-comings and inefficiency of the legal justice system.

My family came to visit me often. My mother came the very night when I had been booked. I cannot quite remember why my father was not with her; I assume it must have been a work meeting, or maybe he was not in town. However, he did come eventually and brought my sister with him. There was a point when I realized that if I had to grade my family members in order of how supportive they were during these trying times, I realized I simply would not be able to. They were all equally supportive, loving, patient and calm.

Not long before, my fellow inmates broke the news to me that Usman was alive and would soon be well. How he survived is borderline mind-blowing. The shot was point-blank, and the chances of survival were slim to none. It turns out that the gun he had pointed at me at the club, his friends had taken it away when shit hit the fence so that Usman would not be to blame in that entire situation.

He was still a gang member today; he walked and talked normally, aside from a very light, noticeable slur. Obviously, he was a lot more cautious and careful when it came to gang-related issues and such. When I first found out that he was alive and well, I felt more glad than pissed because it meant my offence would be a bit less severe. Also, I felt that I had avenged myself, stood up tall, and did my part. More on this later.

Ironically, in both the army and in jail, the constituent humans who are subjected to similar kinds of training or torture acknowledge each other's pain and suffering more empathetically. With this inevitable empathy, they form a bond that is very strong. Simply said, they use each other's company and the bond they have between them as a coping mechanism that gets them through several years of harsh physical and mental conditions. The bond itself perhaps lasts longer than the time they individually spend together in prison. This bond is cultivated into some sort of brotherhood that many look up to. Also, yes, I made many friends and acquaintances in jail. Understand this: Mostly, when gangsters end up in prison, they have previously either messed up big time and have intentionally/unintentionally compromised the integrity of their gang, people who others thought to be goofs or others who have been moles and rats, intentionally nibbling their way out of both, morality and loyalty. In my case, however, the situation was neither. Not only was it unique in its way, but it was also something the prisoners, me, the officers, and much of the public knew about my predicament and could understand and relate to. To all these individuals, I was merely a high school boy who had been unsightly, gruesomely shot and had suffered for many years to no end while my enemies went unpunished until I took matters into my own hands and capitalized on the right opportunity.

To them, I was a hero of sorts who was clearly and efficiently highlighting the shortcomings of the legal justice system by simply existing within its shard-ridden cells of isolation and pain. I was the loophole in Canada's legal system. Because my case was a solid loophole, I was the embodiment of hope. I suppose this was also a big reason why several people had their eyes on the outcome of my case and its proceedings.

The connections I formed in jail were solid and deep, like those in the army. In a way, I suppose it is very similar to high school. Perhaps that is why it was relatively easier for me to survive and low-key thrive here because I was fresh out of high school. Meanwhile, other older offenders who came to jail for the second or third time took a bit of time adjusting to the reality concealed within these thick concrete walls. Some of these connections were superficial; they were nothing but pure entertainment, just like the bond I had with that bike gangster, John Felix.

At one point during my several months in almost complete solitude, I began to realize a creative side of me. It felt like an uncurling octopus of sorts. Initially, I thought it was a mere hobby that manifested due to a lack of activities to keep myself occupied. It was not until after some time had passed that I realized that what I had been channelling onto paper with my pencil was somewhat potent, although it was raw. Down here, in the depths of human solitude and emotional desperation, I was beginning to discover the meaningful potential within me. Not long before, and as corny as it may sound, my pencil and paper became my biggest companions. I channelled my creative energy into making independent comics and began to tell stories in my own unique way. With all the rare and interesting stories alongside the unheard perspectives that I had gathered from my fellow inmates in jail, I had an open mind as my creative juices were brimming. One particular genre in which I fully immersed my mind and heart was dark science fiction. I stand today at a point where I am about to have one such work of mine published soon. There will be a second book coming soon, so fingers crossed.

I would say that for someone who was in jail for quite a long time in their youth, I was pretty well connected with the world outside of jail. Not only did I have many friends who wrote letters to me regularly, like my girls Carla, Linda and Mandy amongst many others, who all wrote letters on the regular, sending me postcards, pictures, and other such memories, but I also wrote back to them and made sure to keep all of them well-informed on how I was doing. Finally, I did join some counselling sessions. There was a psychiatrist who assessed me. At that time, I was not guilty because I had not really been convicted yet. It amazes me still to this day how I spent two whole years of my early twenties cleaning and listening to stories on repeat, then channelling some of the stories that took root deep in my brain onto paper in an artistic manner. We had a prison bookshelf, so I did a lot of reading. I was never the brightest kid at school, and it was maybe because I was free and a part of the world outside. But now, it was me and solitude, which followed me wherever I went, within the prison premises. I had all the time in the world. All I could do was read and write. If I were to describe this new discovery of myself in a nerd-like language, I would say it felt like I had levelled up several notches on the genius scale. It felt as if, not just in terms of street intelligence but also academic sharpness, the jail had taught me in two years what school did not in over 18 years. I indulged head-first into reading quite a lot. Books were interesting and fun, and I used them as a pathway to escapism.

All of a sudden, I had this new world to get rid of all my problems. I wasn't a convict nor guilty and was whatever I wanted to be. A lot of the intellect and knowledge that I now use as an adult is mostly what I have retained from the extensive reading and learning I did during those two years. Within that time, my brain felt like a temple, similar to how Doctor Strange had concealed himself in near-isolation to learn mystic arts. I had been forced into isolation to become a better human being. Even though, justly speaking, it was not a fate that I deserved. The legal system had forced me into isolation in order to succumb to its boundaries and shortcomings, accepting my fate under its realm. All I could do was make lemonade out of the lemons I had.

But again, as the wise would imply, and as all religious and spiritual fanatics would mimic, everything happens for a damn good reason.

Shooter gets six years

Leslie Raymond sentenced to jail for blasting alleged gangster

By TONY BLAIS
Court Bureau

The victim of a 1996 gang shooting bowed his head in court yesterday after being sentenced to six years in prison for shooting an alleged gangster in the face in a crowded city bar.

Leslie Cletus Raymond, 22, pleaded guilty to attempted murder for the March 27, 1999, shooting of Usman Pervez, however Court of Queen's Bench Justice Erik Lefsrud said it was a miracle it wasn't a first-degree murder case.

"In my view it is a miracle that the complainant, who was shot point-blank in the face, is alive today," said Lefsrud. "It's an absolute miracle."

Lefsrud said he accepted there was a history of bad blood between Raymond and Pervez, which allegedly resulted in Raymond being shot five times in the parking lot of Southgate Shopping Centre in 1996.

But the judge said Raymond committed "an inexcusable act" when he pulled out a Colt 45-calibre semi-automatic handgun in front of 370 people at the Windmill Bar and Grill at Millbourne Shopping Centre and shot Pervez, 21.

"There is no excuse for the violent steps that Mr. Raymond took that night," said Lefsrud, adding that it needs to be driven home that "even if you feel frightened or threatened, you don't take the law in your own hands."

Lefsrud said a nine-year prison term was appropriate, but he subtracted two years for the 13.5 months Raymond spent in pretrial custody and one year for his guilty plea.

Raymond apologized for the shooting, but said he just reacted to a death threat from a "bad guy" who continues to this day to vow to finish him off.

Raymond's mother Sheila began crying when sentence was passed, as did other friends and family in court. "There is no justice in this country," she said. "That's all I have to say."

Court heard Raymond was in the Windmill with his girlfriend when Pervez and a group of his friends approached him and taunted and threatened him. Raymond charged towards Pervez and pulled out the gun, which was apparently passed to him from a friend, and shot him in the face. He was nabbed by bar security and held until police arrived.

Pervez ended up with a bullet lodged in his mouth and is missing part of his jaw and several teeth. He needs a bone transplant from his hip to repair the damage, court heard.

Court was told police allege Pervez is the head of a gang called the Browns, who are bitter rivals of a group called the Blacks, of which Raymond is allegedly a member. Raymond denies belonging to a gang.

Defence lawyer Jonathan Healey said the Windmill shooting was the result of "extreme provocation" stemming from when Raymond was shot and nearly killed by an individual associated with Pervez.

A teen was earlier sentenced to 24 months in jail in youth court after pleading guilty to aggravated assault and possession of a restricted weapon for shooting Raymond.

Leslie Raymond
Reacted to threat

EDITOR: Bob Cox, 429-5399; city@thejournal.southam.ca

The Edmonton Journal

NIGHTCLUB SHOOTING

Judge denies bail

KERRY POWELL
LEGAL AFFAIRS WRITER

Edmonton

Leslie Raymond lost his bid for bail Thursday on a charge of attempted murder for allegedly shooting another man in the face.

The Crown and defence lawyers painted very different pictures of Raymond and the March 27 shooting before Assistant Chief Judge Peter Caffaro rejected the 21-year-old's request for house arrest in his parents' home.

Prosecutor Sarah Langley said the "unbelievable" shooting in front of 200 people at a Mill Woods nightclub was part of an ongoing dispute between two groups, the Blacks and the Browns.

She said Raymond belongs to the Blacks and the victim, 20-year-old Usman Pervez, is the leader of the Browns, who has been released from hospital and is still recovering.

The same dispute resulted in Raymond being shot almost three years ago. Langley said Raymond, then 16, was shot in the leg, back, hip and stomach in the parking lot of Southgate Mall on July 5, 1996.

Langley said in Raymond's statement to police in March, he claimed Pervez had harassed him several times since, saying just because

Raymond didn't die, it didn't mean their argument was over.

Raymond told police Pervez confronted him at the Windmill Bar and Grill March 27, "looked at me and said he was going to finish me off."

Please see SHOOTING/B3 back page of this section

Case Book

The accused: Leslie Cletus Raymond, 21, charged with attempted murder, pointing a firearm, possession of a loaded weapon, possession of a restricted weapon with an obliterated serial number and possession of an unlawful firearm.

The allegations: That on March 27 at the Windmill Bar and Grill in Mill Woods, he shot Usman Pervez, 20, in the face and pointed a gun at a bouncer.

The news: A judge denied Raymond's bail Thursday. His next appearance is April 29.

75th in 2010?

ALLAN CHAMBERS
JOURNAL STAFF WRITER

Edmonton

Once the terms of reference have been developed, they will be brought to council for approval,

10

Jail, A Familiar Friend

Even though I was trying my best to focus on the good in life, looking forward to a better future, I could not help but think that my arch-nemesis, whom I put my life on the line to kill, was roaming free and happy, seemingly stronger than before. At this point, he thought he was bulletproof, invincible, untouchable, any possible adjective you could think of that associated with his egoistic self. He had new contacts, new deals, and newer customers because of the fame he gained through the incident in which I nearly killed him, but he somehow survived.

My friends thought I would be angry. But truth be told, I was just deeply disappointed. I felt as if God had let me down. My life was already in the dumps; I had ailments from when this man had sent his minions to pop me with multiple bullets, yet he got to roam as a free man. Fairness and reality seemed two opposite worlds to me, a world where nothing but the free will of men and chaos existed. A world where nothing was predetermined, and it was all in the hands of the men who took charge. Where evil prevailed and goodness submerged. I prayed and did all I could to seek justice, but it seemed like the Big Guy clearly did not want justice served. Despite all the pain I had been through already, it seemed as if there was more. Many would say that my attempt at taking that sinister, rouge bully's life was justified. However, it seemed like God most certainly did not feel that way. Perhaps God wanted me to show patience while he dealt with him through the karma of his own wrongdoings. But it was too late.

Soon enough, I was up for trial. My lawyer came in regularly to try and prepare me for the trial. He also informed me in one of his sessions that Usman would be coming to testify against me during the trial. I do not exactly remember if either my friends or my lawyer informed me of this particular detail. However, I found out that a year before the trial, Usman had been arrested and put in jail for being seized with a pound of marijuana. Truthfully, I did not care what he was arrested for, especially if it was for something as meagre as weed, because he was a far cruder, sinister person than I could ever imagine to be. Yet I was serving time for attempted murder; meanwhile, he might easily get out earlier for mere drug possession. I also came to realize sometime later, that had it not been for him being in jail, he might have not even cared to come to the trial to testify.

Pre-trial, Usman and I came to a close encounter when we were both locked up near one another. Seeing his face painted with that perverse expression that he used to mock me without using little to no words, I absolutely lost my mind. I started screaming at him. I yelled and told him that I did not regret pulling the trigger at all because I would do it time and time again. I kept hollering like a madman who had lost every ounce of sensibility until the guards quieted me down. They explained to me that whatever I said to him now could be used against me in the trial. The guards put me in restraints and kept asking me to calm down. Meanwhile, Usman stood in his holding cell, not uttering a single word yet smirking at me as if he had won this round of the game. It was only two years ago I had shot him right in his face, and his chances of surviving were highly unlikely. Looking at him, it did not seem as if two years had passed. The fact that he had survived was not anything remarkable on his end; he was extremely lucky. However, the atrocious audacity with which he stood smirking at me, tauntingly with his asymmetrical, misaligned face, had me boiling with rage.

When I was brought into trial, the security put me in shackles and all kinds of restraints possible that would only allow me to stand throughout the trial. The guards feared that I would genuinely run across toward Usman, strangle and murder him on the spot if I could. They were certain I would not hesitate if the opportunity came about. Hence, they made me look like an absolute madman in the courtroom. With all the restraints amidst the press coverage, I was not represented aptly. However, it did not matter to me because most of the people who were following my story knew for good reason that my case and situation were a prime example of Canada's judicial system of the time rather than it all being a criminal's atonement for attempted murder.

During the trial, the same bartender was called upon to testify against me. He described in detail how he threw himself between me and the club's exit so that the police could arrive in time to arrest me. He also described how he feared for his life that I might attempt to take his life and shoot him. At that moment, instead of being angry, I truly felt a deep sense of remorse for how I may have seemed threatening and dangerous to the bouncer when he was only doing what any responsible civilian would do. I also personally admitted to myself how I might have shot him given, at that very moment, I had not quite been thinking straight. I did remember firing twice and thinking that I may have hurt another person. Luckily, everyone ran to cover what the incident was unravelling. After the bouncer described the events of that day from his perspective in detail, I struggled to make eye contact with him.

On the other hand, Usman did not say much aside from answering "yes" or "no" to relevant questions. All along, however, he maintained his malevolent smirk while staring at me a good deal of the time as if to provoke me to make one more wrong move. Anything that happened then in court would have possibly wrecked my entire future for me, and he knew it. At that point, however, especially after the bouncer's testimony, I was left with little or no desire for revenge. As if I had seen my reflection, I saw my soul and the monster I had set out to become. This had gone on for far too long and needed to end. I was just your average kid on the block, only to now be a convict for murder, standing at trial while a witness spoke about how he feared I would shoot him. All it takes is one bad day, and that day led me to the man I had become. I did not like this man and wanted to get as far away from him as possible. I had been in jail for two whole years, and I just wanted out. I wanted to go back home to my family and live like an ordinary 20-year-old. I wanted to go to college, major in a discipline that interested me, and be a successful young person who was on his path to setting his career straight.

When the judge was about to announce my sentence, I felt an overwhelming sense of anxiety, and an existential crisis took over me like never before. It was as if my soul had unfurled out of my toes and fingertips, balling up in an extremely uncomfortable way in the core and middle of my gut. My stomach felt heavy as I was on the verge of getting extremely sick. This was it; this was the defining moment of the rest of my life.

The judge turned to me and cut the rope of my fate. He said that he would have given me nine years of jail time, but since I had already spent two years being locked up, he would give me six. However, if I displayed good behavior, I might even get out in two years and stay on probation for the rest of the four.

This news hit me like a bulldozer. While many would have considered the latter part as good news, I could not bear to think of spending six whole years of my short-lived youth behind bars. I was twenty at the time, and I had already spent two years in prison. To top it off, I had to spend more than a quarter of my life in jail. I wanted to throw up, scream, and cry, yet a part of me was also dead. Somehow, even though I hoped for the best possible outcome, our expectations developed from our experiences, and my recent experiences brought me a subconscious feeling lingering in the background that I was not going to make it as a free man. But those are just thoughts and not reality. When I heard it manifest in actuality, that's when it struck me. It was over.

That day had to be the worst day of my life. You could make an argument based on my story that I have had quite a few of those, but I would argue that this was it. It was worse than me getting shot and surviving death, worse than when I went off on my vengeful spree. Worse than the two birthdays I spent alone in jail instead of being with my family. It was worse than the moment in the ambulance when I realized I might not live, as my difficulty in breathing seemed like my last one.

My family was at the trial. I could see the pain in their eyes, even though they did their very best to look and be strong for me. They would write to me later and assure me that it would all work out for the best, that God knew what he was doing, and that it was all for character development and for a far more superior alignment of my life. I wanted to believe them, but at the same time, I could not. It simply felt as if the entire universe was working against me and in favor of the devil's apprentice. I doubted myself and wondered where I had gone wrong and why I was receiving the exact opposite of what I deserved.

After my trial, I was transferred to federal jail. This was quite different from where I had been held previously. Looking back, I realize that, in fact, things had worked out for the better because the time I spent here, believe it or not, was truly well spent. For starters, unlike where I was before, federal jail was medium to low security, which meant that I only had to spend three hours a day locked up. It was funny because I basically slept longer than that. I had a lot more freedom and even had recreational activities that I could do. For example, not only did I have the blessing of being able to get more outdoor time and fresh air, something I had not valued much as a teenager until I was locked away in the grim, depressing dark for about two years. But I also had better library facilities, more time to socialize, food that was slightly better than what I had been eating for the last two years, and even gym facilities. I made the most of my time working out and building gains. There was also hockey, a basketball court, and a tennis court. Sometimes, we would play hockey with some prison guards, who would take some time out for us. It would be us against them, and it was quite fun. I was a good sport, keeping in mind that I worked out and played with a bad leg.

The social aspect of being in federal jail was quite interesting. For the most part, everyone was divided into groups, just like children are in school. Here, inmates associated themselves with groups based on their races or gangs. There had been a cleanout recently, and so a lot of gangs had been taken down by the police and locked up. Aside from these gangs, there were black inmates, Pakistanis, Indians, Aboriginals, Native and Asian groups. I did not associate myself solidly with any group, but I seemed to get the most brotherhood-like treatment from other black guys in jail, which was understandable. Everyone was quite civil to one another because everyone had to be on their best behavior to be able to leave prison earlier than their sentence. In which case, much like what the judge had sentenced me to, they would have to spend the remaining period in their residence on probation.

It was not long after I joined federal jail that I realized that a few of Usman's friends were here too, but I felt no need to quarrel with them. I felt like I had taught myself enough to rise above that anger, so I merely chose to ignore their existence altogether, even though they were my mutual enemies. I met Vincent Gambella again a while ago, and even though he was a badass in his personal life, he seemed to have an odd soft spot for me. He would narrate a lot of gang-related stories for me that I genuinely couldn't care less about yet dared never to express to rub off on his wrong side. Needless to say, I would never associate myself with people like him. Gambella still assured me time and time again that I had his and his people's respect and protection, and if anyone were to come to pick on me, they had my back. Perhaps that was why Usman's friends never attempted to make a move on me. That form of emotion that Gambella and his crew indirectly gave me really humbled and softened me to a point where sometimes I considered this particular jail to be some gray, depressing hostel rather than an actual prison.

Looking back, when I hear children of today talk about their lives in hostels or other such institutionalized units of living, I realize that this inspiration that I had back then of my predicament was correct. It surprises me to this day.

Feelings of anger had started to subside. I was settling in. Obviously, I was not having the time of my life, but I was also not suffering as one would expect in imprisonment. Those crazy stories, sometimes fictionalized, sometimes true, about the man who "purposely went to jail." The story of how the man who was imprisoned and was released, only to realize he had to find and maintain a full-time job to eat, sleep and repeat, was much more demanding than the life he had in prison, and so he found a way to go back there, in what he defines as a place of broken prosperity. I could see how that could happen, and I know not all jails are the same, especially those in third-world countries, but the federal prison I was in wasn't all too bad. If you kept to yourself, carried a small group of friends and stayed far away from the gamblers, you could peacefully do your time. Considering the type of people I was surrounded with, one cannot help but wonder if it was a punishment because it did not quite feel like it. What I'm trying to say is that it wasn't all bad. Maybe because I was young, or perhaps they took some pity, knowing what had happened to me that I didn't deserve to be here. Jail is kinda like a fingerprint where everybody has their own unique experience. I do not know whether to be glad or not. Glad I did not have to go through hell in there, and not so because of all who committed hideous crimes and do not suffer like those who were at the wrong end of their wrath.

11

Liberation

Time had passed, matters had changed, and I had changed. What remained constant during all this time was the 20 grand on my head. I found out later during my time in federal jail that the people who were paying for my execution were none other than Usman and his goons. Though the mention of his name did buzz a triggering fist, Usman and his people had a reputation. When it comes to gang life, your reputation is everything. Be it your corporate life, your past successes, your storyline, or your experience, nothing matters if your reputation does not speak for itself. Reputation is all that matters, particularly in the streets, in order to maintain a respectful and peaceful coexistence with other gangs and such. At the same time, I was respected or ignored by most people. I stayed close to my cellmate Barriffe, a Jamaican dread who was the leader of the Black culture group, and his reputation was solid. Usman and his men had a reputation that was quite the opposite of that. They were known to not hold up to their word or their commitments; a lot of what they said were lies, and not to mention, the biggest and most well-known flaw was that they never paid up.

Not paying up is dangerous for oneself, considering you were paying for murder, to begin with. Usman had already been going around for a little over two years pretending he was invincible because he was deluded by the fact that he survived a gunshot to the face without any extremities. I suppose he thought that incident ought to show everyone else not to mess with him. However, a dog's tail will always be crooked.

At that moment, when I was rotting away in federal jail, I did wonder how people even expected him to go through with the offer of 20 grand. He probably had not even seen 20 grand in his life. It solidified in my head later that this was exactly what Vincent Gambella had been trying to warn me about the first time when I had been booked, the night I shot Usman. He had been telling me subtly since we crossed paths, only in a more indirect manner for obvious reasons. Even though Usman had a reputation that no big gang or name wanted anything to do with, there were still measly and miserable creatures in jail who believed that prize money was real and were desperate enough to do anything. Barriffe had told me to watch out. Alongside him, even the guards knew about the amount on my head and many others who were after it. The irony would show me that Vincent would meet his demise at the hands of his victim's cousin. What goes around comes around was a standard saying in the Big House.

In my two-plus years in prison, bench and shoulder presses paid their due dividend as I had built up a decent physique and had gone bulkier and more muscular. I was healthy, and not only did I progress physically but also academically. During my time in jail, I spent a great deal of time in the library writing and reading, sharpening my brain. So, I redid school, upgraded my classes, and got my GED. I finished school and was a stellar student in all my classes. I visited correction facilities often to keep my nose clean and dove headfirst into a much better, productive, and progressive lifestyle. It really was for the best, and my life took a sharp turn, which I needed so desperately. Safe to say, I emerged not just a new leaf but a productive, proactive member of a constructive society.

Even the psychologist I visited for scheduled assessments had quite a bit to say about how I had absolutely no major problems aside from mild anger issues that he put me on track to control. He had seen his fair share of crazy, having to assess criminals and had blatantly told me that I should not even be in jail in the first place.

One morning, while I was serving my time, quite a while later, I recall watching television, only to find the truly devastating news that Usman's brother Adnan had been murdered. The details of the case were a bit jarring and depressing to me. The boy had grown up idolizing his unethical, corrupt and underhanded brother, who was not even fit or remotely admirable for gang standards, let alone anything else. And for such liking and idolization, the boy paid with his life. It seemed as if Usman was so lucky in his choices and dwellings that it was all a curse. All the people in his family had paid big time on his behalf. Adnan's story had me quite emotional because it had quite literally happened at the front of their mother's parking lot. He was taking out the trash when a car pulled up and gunned him down in front of his house. Everyone had suffered gravely but Usman, who lives to this day. Karma definitely worked its way through the natural happenstances of life. However, I don't know if Usman ever perceived it that way.

Suddenly, after internalizing the shock and sadness of his brother's death, I came to realize another horrifying fact: everyone's eyes were now on me. Everyone, including gangsters in and out of jail, was thinking that I had some of my links murder Usman's little brother. At that moment, not only did I know that this situation would be hard to put behind me, but I also realized a new sense of fear. There had already been a large sum on my head. Still, recent events have added heat to the conversation, and this might trigger some violent, dangerous activity either directly from Usman or his men. I thought he might get one of his men to be jailed with the intent of my murder. No one at that point quite knew who the murderer was and which gang they belonged to. It was later uncovered that Usman's problematic gang had dug rifts with their own people, a gang of Sikhs in particular, who was responsible for Adnan's murder.

Eventually, I was up for parole, and much to my relief and years of hope, I was given parole. Finally, after four long years of being behind bars, I was a free man. I spent my late teens and the start of my twenties in jail in a dark, depressing cell and in the company of criminals. This was the age when people went out and partied the hardest right before having to take the reins of their lives and slow down to set a more serious purpose for their living, education, and finances. I had missed the opportunity to do so, but in my own personal opinion, I do not regret being behind bars during my maturing phase. If I was not sent to jail, who knows? I probably would still have been involved in gang activities, and my life would have been a complete rut.

My parents came to pick me up, and I was assigned to leave home that day. Knowing the kind of eventful life I have lived from a young age, this day was definitely the happiest of all my days. I will never forget that feeling of walking out of prison, knowing I may possibly never have to come to this place ever again.

Shortly after I was released, a shooting incident occurred at a Sikh gang leader's house, with two casualties as an outcome, including the gang leader himself. Even though most of the individuals who were involved in rifts with Usman and the likes of him were all youngsters, the people who fell victim to the shootings in this incident were older men, too, one being around 53, I suppose. Because of this incident, Usman was once again arrested. He had sent out men to kill the leader of the Sikh gang and to send out a message. Despite the fact that Usman and I went way back and that he had taken almost everything away from me, he could not kill me. In this situation, I took from the example of this Sikh leader and was pretty grateful for not only being alive but being a much better and improved version of myself.

It was when I came out of jail that Usman and his men were being sent to prison for a charge far more extreme than mine, first-degree murder. My dear readers, there is great power and wisdom in this. I finally felt peace knowing that this had all worked out for the better. I soon heard that he had been plotting against me even though he could not directly get to me himself. However, gladly so, sometime after Usman was convicted and right before he went up for trial, his gang put a final end to our years-long rift.

I was eating out with my friends at a nice restaurant when his people approached me in an almost threatening manner. Their presence, not to mention the fact that they wanted a word with me, was uneasy. Though I was not scared of them, it was a blast for a past I was not keen on revisiting. Also, what shocked me was not them but my own rage. I did not trust myself enough to be around these guys. I feared they might say something with their combined IQ of about 50, which would, in turn, make me make a decision for the worst. As much as I hated Usman and his men and wanted the man who disabled me dead, I was not desperate enough to end up in jail once again.

I told them to come back later because I was with young Southside, Jomo's younger brother and crew. Some of them even teamed up with Tin and were well-connected. The Southside made sure everything was going to stay neutral. We surrounded them, and I could have done the most, but I didn't. Shockingly, I learned that Usman's men were there to not get back at me for anything. They were there to officially talk it out and put behind all past rifts that my homies and they ever had. They told me how both Usman and I were even, and it was in everyone's best interest to move on.

Usman went on trial and was convicted for life. Everything that happened was such a long time ago that I often feel disconnected from such parts of my life. So detached; it feels like a memory from a past life rather than all having occurred in this lifetime. After becoming a free man once again, I joined my father at his company, fell in love, had a child, and helped raise him. I got my life back on the right track with a few stumbles along the way. Navigating my new life forward shall be interesting with my new friends Tamara and Richard. After this incident my city had adopted numerous gun violence that has left scars on our city streets. I made a silent vow to myself to turn over a new leaf and grow from this profound life lesson of violence. Now that I have my child Emsco to protect from the horrors of this world, I not only look back on the sacrifices and fears of my parents in a new light but with a newfound appreciation for life itself.

The Edmonton Sun, Monday, June 16, 2003   NEWS 7

A KILLER'S SHRUG

Usman Pervez
Raised eyebrows

Pair far from shocked by murder convictions

By TONY BLAIS
Court Bureau

Raised eyebrows and a shrug of shoulders is how two killers reacted last night when a jury convicted them of first-degree murder for a Mill Woods contract slaying.

Neither Usman Pervez, 24, nor Mike Debrocke, 21, seemed shocked by the verdict of the eight-woman, four-man jury, but the younger triggerman was definitely ghostly pale and the man who hired him appeared a little upset.

As the jury chairman forcefully stated "guilty" to convict Pervez of hiring Debrocke to shoot Ranjit Mangat, 22, in a retaliation killing to avenge the earlier shooting of his brother Adnan, 18, Pervez raised his eyebrows.

He then turned in the prisoners box to face Debrocke, who resignedly shrugged his shoulders, and mouthed what looked to be a one-word obscenity.

Just before handing the killers the mandatory life sentence, Court of Queen's Bench Justice Sterling Sanderman remarked how anticlimactic it is when someone is convicted of the most serious crime there is.

"The two of you have been convicted of first-degree murder and it is my duty to sentence you to life in prison with no eligibility of parole for 25 years," said Sanderman.

The judge also ordered the pair to submit a sample of their DNA for the national DNA data bank in Ottawa and handed them a life-time weapons prohibition.

Surprisingly, neither the parents of Pervez nor the mother of Debrocke were present for the verdict, despite attending the majority of the month-long trial.

As Pervez was led away by court constables, he gave a big smile to Const. Kevin Brezinski, of the city police gang unit, who was sitting in court with a homicide detective.

During the trial Brezinski testified about a war between two feuding rival Mill Woods groups, one of which Pervez headed, and described a litany of drive-by shootings, Molotov cocktail attacks and parent-issued truces culminating in the Dec. 13, 2000, slaying of Adnan Pervez.

Brezinski said Pervez was very upset after his brother was gunned down in the driveway of their family's Mill Woods home and told him he believed it was a contract hit ordered by Ranjodh Mangat and his cousin Ranjit.

Brezinski testified Pervez told him in January 2001 he would let police handle the case, but a month later stated: "But if you don't do your job, then we decide what to do."

Mangat was shot four times through the torso and three times in the head on March 27, 2001, in the driveway of his family's 4532 27 Ave. house by a man who ran out from the backyard as Mangat came home with two female cousins.

Desmond Thomas, a 19-year-old man who confessed he was the getaway driver, testified Debrocke was the shooter and Pervez set up the killing, even co-ordinating the hit by issuing instructions from nearby via walkie-talkie.

In an elaborate undercover police sting operation in which officers pretended they were part of a phony crime syndicate, Debrocke was tricked into confessing details of the shooting for which he says he was paid $20,000.

The Crown also provided the jury with evidence of cellphone records, surveillance and wiretapped conversations to illustrate the contract retaliation killing.

Kalla Mussell, inset, never shed a tear. The Chilliwack, B.C., saddle-bronc rider never made the whistle during last night's performance at the Daines Ranch Rodeo, near Innisfail. But she won respect. The 24-year-old cowgal battled bronc Farmer Joe for five seconds before going over the top for a not-so-graceful face plant, left. Gutsy Mussell got up, wiped the mud off her face and acknowleged the crowd of 1,200 that gave her a standing ovation.

— KEVIN UDAHL, Sun Media photos

Cord-tangle toddler fights for her life

By PAUL COWAN
Staff Writer

A toddler remained fighting for her life in pediatric intensive care last night after being strangled by the cord from a blind.

The 15-month-old girl was found lifeless and tangled up in the cord in a bedroom in her parent's apartment at Bellamy Plaza, 9915 Bellamy Hill, shortly after 7 p.m. Tuesday.

"I can speak for the entire Emergency Response Department when I say our thoughts and prayers are with the family," operations Supt. Rick Crane said yesterday.

circulating to the brain.

A fire crew was the first emergency team to reach the apartment.

"They were closest and they have basic medical training," explained spokesman Karen Carlson.

"Time is critical in situations like this."

Paramedics then arrived and launched into their advanced resuscitation and life support procedures.

By the time the toddler reached the Stollery Children's Hospital, her heart was beating on its own.

"The crews carry a special pediatric re-
"They aren't just small adults and have special medical needs. The drugs used in the resuscitation and the dosages involved are different."

The department has counsellors who can help emergency crews deal with the stresses connected with particularly distressing calls.

O'Keefe said the 911 dispatchers are issued with cards with advice on how to deal with various medical emergencies which are kept close at hand for such situations.

Last night the toddler's condition was listed as critical.

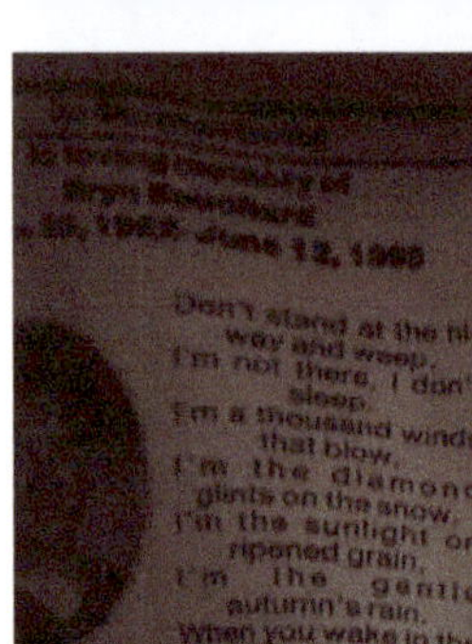

Shooting was bloody climax to years of ill will in Mill Woods

MURDER
Continued from B1

Defence lawyers called his comments boasting, not a confession. They also cast doubt on the reliability of key testimony from witnesses such as Thomas, saying police drilled into him that they thought Pervez was involved.

"The police had a theory and they did everything they could to make the evidence fit their theory," defence lawyer Rod Gregory argued.

Neither of the accused testified.

The shooting was the bloody climax to years of ill will between groups of Sikh and Muslim Mill Woods youths that apparently started in junior high school.

With any luck, that's now over.

Since Mangat was shot, police aren't "aware of any incidents of violence involving these two groups," police spokesman Sgt. Chris Hayden said Wednesday.

"The beef between them is more of a rivalry than anything else. There's no religious significance or drug dealing."

The Mangat house on 45th Street near 27th Avenue was firebombed in August 2000 and hit with bullets during a drive-by shooting.

It was one of seven similar incidents that month before parents of the groups, including the Mangat and Pervez families, met to arrange a truce.

Pervez is no stranger to trouble. In

OTHER CONVICTIONS

■ Keith Schell, 38, was found guilty of first-degree murder last October for gunning down 18-year-old Adnan Pervez in December 2000. His target was Adnan's brother, Usman.

■ Schell, a cocaine addict who carried out the killing so he would have Christmas money, was given the mandatory sentence of life in prison with no parole eligibility for 25 years. His conviction is under appeal.

■ Edmond "Jackie" So, 25, pleaded guilty to conspiracy to commit murder for helping find someone to kill Usman. He was sentenced to 12 years in prison.

■ Michael Debrocke and Usman Pervez still face charges of conspiracy to commit murder. They are set to return to court Aug. 13.

March 1999, he was shot in the mouth with a .45-calibre handgun at a Mill Woods nightclub.

The bullet knocked out teeth and lodged near his spine, but he miraculously avoided serious, long-term injuries.

He had exchanged words earlier in the evening with his assailant, Leslie Raymond, who had been shot outside Southgate Mall in 1996 and thought Pervez was involved.

Raymond later pleaded guilty to attempted murder.

Pervez was sentenced in October 1999 to eight months in jail for selling a half-kilogram of marijuana.

At the time, lawyer Walter Raponi said he was a changed man, leaving a life of crime to help run his family's business, setting up dollar stores.

While Raponi called him a "Jekyll and Hyde" personality who could be pleasant with some people and get in trouble with others, a probation officer described him as a "charismatic con artist."

The two men will return to court Aug. 13 to face charges of conspiracy to commit murder.

ghent@thejournal.canwest.com

'I don't believe most Albertans are intolerant'

SIMONS

riage would neither threaten heterosexual marriage nor infringe on the religious freedom of churches, synagogues, mosques and temples which do not matter.

We don't protect minority rights through popularity polls but through the rule of law. The majority of people in Selma in the 1960s didn't favour racial in-

---

Life for murderers of Mangat

Upon sentencing, killers look at each other and shrug

GORDON KENT
Legal Affairs Writer
EDMONTON

The long, violent feud that terrorized Mill Woods residents for more than a year came to a close Wednesday when two men were convicted of murdering a rival.

Usman Pervez and Michael Debrocke were immediately sentenced for first-degree murder after a jury found them both responsible in the death of Ranjit Mangat, 22.

Mangat was shot seven times outside his family's home March 27, 2001, by a lone gunman carrying a Glock pistol.

Both men will serve automatic life sentences, with no chance of parole for 25 years. They are also prohibited from ever possessing firearms or explosives and must submit samples of their DNA to a government registry.

When the jury's forewoman read the verdict after a day and a half of deliberations, Pervez and Debrocke turned to look at each other, tilting their heads sideways. Pervez raised his eyebrows and shrugged.

His lawyers declined to comment.

Crown prosecutor Marilena Carminati said it would not be appropriate for her to comment since Pervez and Debrocke still have 30 days to appeal.

Evidence during the five-week trial indicated the killing was an act of revenge.

Pervez, 24, felt Mangat was part of a Sikh group behind the murder of his brother Adnan, who had been gunned down three months earlier outside the Pervez family home.

While Pervez, apparently the real target of the hit, gave tips to police officers trying to solve Adnan's slaying, he was also devising his own plan for retaliation.

He paid Debrocke, a former employee at his Calgary dollar store, $20,000 cash to do the hit, and arranged to have the getaway van stolen from a High River Toyota dealership.

Debrocke, 21, and van driver Desmond Thomas watched Mangat's home for three days to learn his schedule before they struck.

Pervez and Debrocke used walkie-talkies to communicate as the murder went down in front of two teenage cousins Mangat had just driven home from work.

As he lay dying on the driveway, Debrocke ran down the street and fled in the van with Thomas to Calgary.

Pervez soon left the country, returning that summer to live in Vancouver, Ontario and Regina.

Debrocke hid out in British Columbia, blowing the money he was paid. In November 2001, he told the story to undercover Calgary police officers he thought were criminals checking him out for membership in their gang.

See MURDER / B9

10 years in prison for 'horrendous offence' at acreage

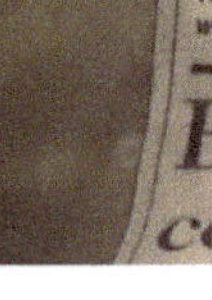

BUBBLES OF FUN

Epilogue

We have all been in situations where we felt the need to say something or do something when someone says or does something to us. We don't want to lose; we don't want to feel afraid, and we don't want to be less than anyone else. But that is and will never be what God wanted from his creations. He made us and put us in this world as a test to see who does what he told us to do and who goes south. Those who do what they were told will never succumb to any man, and justice will be served. But those who operate solely on self-belief, forgetting everything they were sent in this world for, will always lose the battle, even though they might win some wars. For what happened to me, God was always going to respond. I did not have to go to jail. I was not supposed to, yet I did because I took matters into my own hands. Though it is not something I regret, as this is what made me who I am today, it does not mean that others have to make the same mistake. Some tell their story to seek validation. I am a man already validated. I wanted to write this book to tell others who still have a chance, who can learn from my mistakes and show the world that contrary to what some believe, God is very real and brings justice to those who believe in Him who created them. The suffering I endured did not have to be as such if I made the right decision. My nemesis would eventually, as we learned, be held responsible for his crimes. I was a young boy with boiling blood for the injustice that happened to me, and I wanted to do what was right. But what I did was not right. Dear readers, never take justice into your own hands. Trust the process. Trust God.

"Bless those who persecute you; bless and do not curse. Do not repay anyone evil for evil. Do not take revenge, my dear friends, but leave room for God's wrath, for it is written: "It is mine to avenge; I will repay," **Roman 12:19**